ONG

		23/08/16
		27 JAN 2010
	-2 MAY 2006	29 MAY 2018
23 APR 2005		
22 OCT 2009	22 MAR 2007	22 OCT 2019
19 JAN 2006	27 JAN 2009	
16 MAR 2006	12 JAN 12	
	-2 JAN 2016	

This book is to be returned on or before the date above.
It may be borrowed for a further period if not in demand.

Essex County Council
Libraries

30130 139607898

ALSO BY W. SOMERSET MAUGHAN

The Moon and Sixpence
Of Human Bondage
The Narrow Corner
The Razor's Edge
Cakes and Ale
The Summing Up
Collected Stories Vol. 1
Collected Stories Vol. 2
Collected Stories Vol. 3
Collected Stories Vol. 4
Ashenden
Far Eastern Tales
South Sea Tales
For Services Rendered
The Merry-Go-Round
Don Fernando
On a Chinese Screen
The Painted Veil
Catalina
Mrs Craddock
Ten Novels and their Authors
A Writer's Notebook
The Casuarina Tree
Christmas Holiday
Liza of Lambeth
The Magician
Points of View
Selected Plays
Theatre
Then and Now

W. Somerset Maugham

UP AT THE VILLA

ESSEX COUNTY LIBRARY

Published by Vintage 2004

2 4 6 8 10 9 7 5 3 1

Copyright © by the Royal Literary Fund

This book is sold subject to the condition that it shall not by way of trade or otherwise, be lent, resold, hired out, or otherwise circulated without the publisher's prior consent in any form of binding or cover other than that in which it is published and without a similar condition including this condition being imposed on the subsequent purchaser

First published in Great Britain in 1941 by
William Heinemann Ltd

First published by Vintage in 2000

Vintage
Random House, 20 Vauxhall Bridge Road,
London SW1V 2SA

Random House Australia (Pty) Limited
20 Alfred Street, Milsons Point, Sydney
New South Wales 2061, Australia

Random House New Zealand Limited
18 Poland Road, Glenfield,
Auckland 10, New Zealand

Random House (Pty) Limited
Endulini, 5A Jubilee Road, Parktown 2193,
South Africa

The Random House Group Limited Reg. No. 954009
www.randomhouse.co.uk/vintage

A CIP catalogue record for this book
is available from the British Library

ISBN 0 099 47832 3

Papers used by Random House are natural, recyclable products made from wood grown in sustainable forests. The manufacturing processes conform to the environmental regulations of the country of origin

Printed and bound in Great Britain by
Cox & Wyman Limited, Reading, Berkshire

I

The villa stood on the top of a hill. From the terrace in front of it you had a magnificent view of Florence; behind was an old garden, with few flowers, but with fine trees, hedges of cut box, grass walks and an artificial grotto in which water cascaded with a cool, silvery sound from a cornucopia. The house had been built in the sixteenth century by a noble Florentine, whose impoverished descendants had sold it to some English people, and it was they who had lent it for a period to Mary Panton. Though the rooms were large and lofty, it was of no great size and she managed very well with the three servants they had left her. It was somewhat scantily furnished with fine old furniture and it had an air; and though there was no central heating, so that when she had arrived at the end of March it had been still bitterly cold, the Leonards, its owners, had put in bathrooms and it was comfortable enough to live in. It was June now and Mary spent most of the day, when she was at home, on the terrace from which she could see the domes and towers of Florence, or in the garden behind.

For the first few weeks of her stay she had spent much time seeing the sights; she passed pleasant mornings at the Uffizi and the Bargello. She visited the churches and wandered at random in old streets, but now she seldom went down to Florence except to lunch or dine with friends. She was satisfied to lounge about the garden and read books, and if she wanted to go out she preferred to get into the Fiat and explore the country round about. Nothing could have been more lovely with its sophisticated innocence than that Tuscan scene. When the fruit trees were in blossom and when the poplars burst into leaf, their fresh colour crying aloud amid the grey evergreen of the olives, she had felt a lightness of spirit she had thought never to feel again. After the tragic death of her husband, a year before, after the anxious months when she had to be always on hand in case the lawyers who were gathering together what was left of his squandered fortune wanted to see her, she had been glad to accept the Leonards' offer of this grand old house so that she could rest her nerves and consider what she should do with her life. After eight years of extravagant living, and an unhappy marriage, she found herself at the age of thirty with some fine pearls and an income just large enough, with rigid economy, for her support. Well, that was better than it had looked at first when the lawyers, with glum faces, had told her that after the debts were paid they were afraid that nothing would be left at all. At this moment, with two and a half months in Florence behind her, she felt that she could have faced even that prospect with serenity. When she left England the lawyer, an old man and an old friend, had patted her hand.

'Now you've got nothing to worry about, my dear',

he said, 'except to get back your health and strength. I don't say anything about your looks because nothing affects them. You're a young woman and a very pretty one, and I have no doubt you'll marry again. But don't marry for love next time; it's a mistake; marry for position and companionship.'

She laughed. She had had a bitter experience and had no intention then of ever hazarding again the risks of wedlock; it was odd that now she was contemplating doing exactly what the shrewd old lawyer had advised. It looked indeed as though she would have to make up her mind that very afternoon. Edgar Swift was even then on his way to the villa. He had called up a quarter of an hour before to say that he had unexpectedly to go to Cannes to meet Lord Seafair and was starting at once, but urgently wanted to see her before he went. Lord Seafair was the Secretary of State for India and this sudden summons could only mean that Edgar was after all going to be offered the distinguished position upon which he had set his heart. Sir Edgar Swift, K.C.S.I., was in the Indian Civil Service, as her father had been, and he had had a distinguished career. He had been for five years Governor of the North West Provinces and during a period of great unrest had conducted himself with conspicuous ability. He had finished his term with the reputation of being the most capable man in India. He had proved himself a great administrator; though resolute he was tactful, and if he was peremptory he was also generous and moderate. The Hindus and the Muslims liked and trusted him. Mary had known him all her life. When her father died, still a young man, and she and her mother had returned to England, Edgar Swift, whenever he came home on leave, spent a great part of his time with them. As a child he took her to the pantomime or the circus; as a girl in her teens, to the pictures or to the theatre; he sent her presents for her birthday and at Christmas. When she was nineteen her mother had said to her:

'I wouldn't see too much of Edgar if I were you, darling. I don't know if you've noticed it, but he's in love with you.'

Mary laughed.

'He's an old man.'

'He's forty-three', her mother answered tartly.

But he had given her some beautiful Indian emeralds when two years later she married Matthew Panton, and when he had discovered that her marriage was unhappy he had been wonderfully kind. On the expiration of his term as Governor he had gone to London and finding she was in Florence he had come down to pay her a brief visit. He had stayed week after week and Mary would have been a fool not to see that he was waiting for the favourable moment to ask her to marry him. How long had he been in love with her? Looking back, she thought it was ever since she was fifteen, when he had come home on leave and found her no longer a child but a young girl. It was rather touching, that long fidelity. And of course there was a difference between the girl of nineteen, the man of forty-three; and the woman of thirty, the man of fifty-four. The disparity seemed much less. And he was no longer an unknown Indian civilian; he was a man of consequence. It was absurd to suppose that the Government would be content to dispense with his services; he was certainly destined to hold positions of increasing importance. Mary's mother was dead too now, she had no other relations in the world; there was no one of whom she was so fond as of Edgar.

'I wish I could make up my mind', she said.

He couldn't be long now. She wondered whether she should receive him in the drawing-room of the villa, mentioned in the guide-books for its frescoes by the younger Ghirlandaio, with its stately Renaissance furniture and its magnificent candelabra; but it was a formal, sumptuous room, and she felt it would give the occasion an awkward solemnity: it would be better to wait for him on the terrace where she was fond of sitting towards evening to enjoy the view of which she never tired. It seemed a little more casual. If he were really going to ask her to marry him, well, it would make it easier for both of them, out in the open air, over a cup of tea, while she was nibbling a scone. The setting was seemly and not unduly romantic. There were orange trees in tubs and marble sarcophagi brimming over with gaily wanton flowers. The terrace was protected by an old stone balustrade on which at intervals were great stone vases and at each end a somewhat battered statue of a baroque saint.

Mary lay down in a long cane chair and told Nina, the maid, to bring tea. Another chair waited for Edgar.

There was not a cloud in the sky, and the city below, in the distance, was bathed in the soft clear brilliance of the June afternoon. She heard a car drive up. A moment later, Ciro, the Leonards' manservant and Nina's husband, ushered Edgar on to the terrace. Tall and spare, in his well-cut blue serge and a black Homburg, he looked both athletic and distinguished. Even had she not known, Mary would have guessed that he was a good tennis player, a fine rider and an excellent shot. Taking off his hat he displayed a thick head of black curling hair hardly touched with grey. His face was bronzed by he Indian sun, a lean face with a strong chin and an aquiline nose; his brown eyes under the heavy brows were deep-set and vigilant. Fifty-four? He did not look a day more than forty-five. A handsome man in the prime of life. He had dignity without arrogance. He inspired you with confidence. Here was a fellow whom no predicament could perplex and no accident discompose. He wasted no time on small talk.

'Seafair called me on the 'phone this morning and definitely offered me the governorship of Bengal. They've made up their minds that in view of the circumstances they don't want to bring out a man from England who would have to learn the conditions before he could be of use, but someone who is already familiar with them.'

'Of course you accepted.'

'Of course. It's the job of all others that I wanted.'

'I'm so glad.'

'But there are various things to discuss and I've

arranged to go to Milan this evening and get a 'plane from there to Cannes. I shall be away two or three days, which is a bore, but Seafair was anxious that we should meet at once.'

'That's only natural.'

A pleasing smile broke on his firm, somewhat thin-lipped mouth and his eyes shone softly.

'You know, my dear, this is a very important position I'm going to take up. If I make a success of it, it'll be, well, rather a feather in my cap.'

'I'm sure you'll make a success of it.'

'It means a lot of work and a lot of responsibility. But that's what I like. Of course it has its compensations. The Governor of Bengal lives in a good deal of state and I don't mind telling you that that somewhat appeals to me. It's a fine house he lives in too, almost a palace. I shall have to do a lot of entertaining.'

She saw what this was leading to, but looked at him with a bright, sympathetic smile on her lips, as though she had no notion. She was pleasantly excited.

'Of course a man ought to have a wife for a job like that', he went on. 'It's very difficult for a bachelor.'

Her eyes were wonderfully candid when she replied.

'I'm quite sure there are plenty of eligible females who would be glad to share your grandeur.'

'I haven't lived in India for nearly thirty years without having a pretty shrewd suspicion that there's something in what you say. The unfortunate thing is that there's only one eligible female that I would ever dream of asking to do that.'

Now it was coming. Should she say yes or no? Oh dear, oh dear, it was very difficult to make up one's mind. He gave her a glance that was slightly arch.

'Am I telling you something you don't know when I tell you that I've been head over heels in love with you since you were a kid with bobbed hair?'

What did one say to that? One laughed brightly.

'Oh, Edgar, what nonsense you talk.'

'You're the most beautiful creature I've ever seen in my life and the most delightful. Of course I knew I hadn't a chance. I was twenty-five years older than you. A contemporary of your father's. I had a pretty shrewd suspicion that when you were a girl you looked upon me as a funny old fogey.'

'Never', cried Mary, not quite truthfully.

'Anyway, when you fell in love it was natural enough that it should be with someone of your own generation. I ask you to believe me when I tell you that when you wrote and told me you were going to be married I only hoped you would be very happy. I was miserable when I discovered you weren't.'

'Perhaps Mattie and I were too young to marry.'

'A lot of water has flown under the bridges since then. I was wondering if now the discrepancy of our ages seemed as important to you as it did then.'

That was such a difficult question to answer that Mary thought it much better to say nothing but leave him to continue.

'I've always taken care to keep myself pretty fit, Mary. I don't feel my age. But the worst of it is the years have had no effect on you except to make you more beautiful than ever.'

She smiled.

'Is it possible that you're a little nervous, Edgar? That's something I never expected to see you. You, the man of iron.'

'You're a little monster. But you're quite right, I am nervous; and so far as the man of iron is concerned, no one knows better than you that in your hands I've never been anything but a lump of putty.'

'Am I right in thinking that you're proposing to me?'

'Quite right. Are you shocked or surprised?'

'Certainly not shocked. You know, Edgar, I'm very fond of you. I think you're the most wonderful man I've ever known. I'm terribly flattered that you should want to marry me.'

'Then will you?'

There was a curious sense of apprehension in her heart. He was certainly very handsome. It would be thrilling to be the wife of the Governor of Bengal and very nice to be grand and to have A.D.C.s running about to do one's bidding.

'You say you'll be away two or three days?'

'Three at the outside. Seafair has to go back to London.'

'Will you wait for an answer till you come back?'

'Of course. In the circumstances I think it's very reasonable. I'm sure it's much better that you should know your own mind, and I take it that if you definitely knew the answer would be "No" – you wouldn't have to think it over.'

'That's true', she smiled.

'Then we'll leave it at that. I'm afraid I must go now if I don't want to miss my train.'

She walked with him to his taxi.

'By the way, have you told the Princess you wouldn't be able to go to-night?'

They had both been going to a dinner party which the old Princess San Ferdinando was giving that evening.

'Yes, I called her up and told her that I was obliged to leave Florence for a few days.'

'Did you tell her why?'

'You know what an old tyrant she is', he smiled indulgently. 'She told me off good and proper for throwing her over at the last moment and in the end I had to confess the truth.'

'Oh, well, she'll find someone to take your place', Mary replied casually.

'I trust you'll take Ciro with you as I shan't be able to come and fetch you.'

'I can't. I told Ciro and Nina that they could go out.'

'I think it's terribly unsafe for you to drive along these deserted roads by yourself at all hours of the night. But you'll keep your promise to me, won't you?'

'What promise? Oh, the revolver. I think it's perfectly ridiculous, the roads of Tuscany are just as safe as the roads of England, but if it'll set your mind at ease I'll take it with me to-night.'

Knowing how fond Mary was of driving about the country by herself, and having the Englishman's belief that foreigners on the whole were very dangerous people, Edgar had insisted on lending her a revolver and exacted a promise from her that unless she were only going into Florence she would always take it with her.

'The country's full of starving workmen and penniless refugees', he said. 'I shan't have a moment's peace unless I know that if the need arises you can take care of yourself.'

The manservant was at the taxi to open the door for him. Edgar took a fifty-lira note out of his pocket and gave it to him.

'Look here, Ciro, I'm going away for a few days. I shan't be able to come for the Signora to-night. Be sure she takes the revolver when she goes out in the car. She's promised me she would.'

'Very good, Signore', said the man.

2

Mary was doing her face. Nina stood behind her watching with interest and offering now and then unsolicited advice. Nina had been with the Leonards long enough to speak a certain amount of English and Mary in the five months she had lived at the villa had learnt a good deal of Italian, so they got on very well together.

'D'you think I've put on enough rouge, Nina?' asked Mary.

'With the beautiful colour the Signora has naturally I don't know why she wants to put any rouge on at all.'

'The other women at the party will be plastered with it, and if I don't put on a little I shall look like death.'

She slipped into her pretty frock, put on the various bits and pieces of jewellery she had decided to wear, and then perched on her head a tiny, quite ridiculous, but very smart hat. For it was to be that sort of party. They were going to a new restaurant on one of the banks of the Arno where the food was supposed to be very good and where, sitting in the open, they could enjoy the balmy June night and when the moon rose the lovely view of the old houses on the opposite side of the river. The old Princess had discovered a singer there whose voice she thought unusual and whom she wanted her guests to hear.

Mary took up her bag.

'Now I'm ready.'

'The Signora has forgotten the revolver.'

It lay on the dressing-table.

Mary laughed.

'You idiot, that's just what I was trying to do. What is the use of it? I've never fired a revolver in my life and I'm scared to death of it. I haven't got a licence and if I were found with it I should get into all sorts of trouble.'

'The Signora promised the Signore she'd take it.'

'The Signore is an old silly.'

'Men are when they're in love', said Nina sententiously.

Mary looked away. That wasn't a matter she wished to go into just then; Italian servants were admirable, loyal and hard-working, but it was no good to delude yourself with the belief that they didn't know all your business, and Mary was well aware that Nina would be perfectly willing to discuss the whole matter with her in the frankest possible way. She opened her bag.

'All right. Put the beastly thing in.'

Ciro had brought the car round. it was a convertible coupé that Mary had bought when she took the villa and which she was proposing to sell for what it would fetch when she left. She stepped in, drove cautiously along the narrow drive, out of the iron gates and down a winding country lane till she got on to the highway that led into Florence. She turned the light on to see what the time was and finding that she had plenty kept to a leisurely speed. At the back of her mind was a faint disinclination to arrive, for really she would have much preferred to dine by herself on the terrace of the villa. To dine there on a June evening, when it was still day, and after dinner to sit till the softness of the night gradually enveloped her, was a delight of which Mary felt that she could never tire. It gavc her a delicious feeling of peace, but not of an empty peace in which there was something lethargic, of an active, thrilling peace rather in which her brain was all alert and her senses quick to respond. Perhaps it was something in that light Tuscan air that affected you so that even physical sensation had in it something spiritual. It gave you just the same emotion as listening to the music of Mozart, so melodious and so gay, with its undercurrent of melancholy, which filled you with so great a contentment that you felt as though the flesh had no longer any hold on you. For a few blissful minutes you were purged of all grossness and the confusion of life was dissolved in perfect loveliness.

'I was a fool to go', Mary said out loud. 'I ought to have cried off when Edgar was called away.'

But of course that would have been silly. Still, she would have given a good deal to have that evening to herself so that she could think things over quietly. Though she had long guessed Edgar's intentions she had not till that afternoon been quite sure that he would ever bring himself to the point of speaking, and till he did she had felt it unnecessary to make up her mind what she should answer. She would leave it then to the impulse of the moment. Well, now he had, and she felt more hopelessly undecided than before. But by this time she had reached the city, and the crowds of people walking in the roadway, the string of cyclists, forced her to give all her attention to her driving.

When Mary reached the restaurant, she found that she was the last to arrive. The Princess San Ferdinando was American; an elderly woman with iron-grey, tightly waved hair and an authoritative manner, who had lived in Italy for forty years without ever going back to her native country; her husband, a Roman prince, had been dead for a quarter of a century and she had two sons in the Italian army. She had little money, but a caustic tongue and great good-nature. Though she could never have been beautiful and now, with her upright carriage, fine eyes and determined features, was probably better-looking than she had ever been in her youth, she was reported to have been very unfaithful to the prince; but this had not affected the great position she had made for herself; she knew everybody she wished to know and everybody was pleased to know her. The rest of the party consisted of a couple of travelling English people, Colonel and Lady Grace Trail, a sprinkling of Italians and a young Englishman called Rowley Flint. Mary during her stay in Florence had got to know him pretty well. He had indeed been paying her a good deal of attention.

'I must tell you that I'm only a stop-gap', he said when Mary shook hands with him.

'It was unusually nice of him', the Princess put in. 'I asked him when Sir Edgar called up to say he had to go to Cannes and he broke another engagement to come to me.'

'You know quite well I'd break any engagement in the world to come and dine with you, Princess', he said.

The Princess smiled dryly.

'I think I should tell you that he wanted to know exactly who was going to be here before he accepted.'

'It's flattering that we met with his approval,' said Mary.

The Princess gave him another of those quiet smiling looks of hers in which there was the indulgence of an old rip who has neither forgotten nor repented of her naughty past and at the same time the shrewdness of a woman who knows the world like the palm of her hand and come to the conclusion that no one is any better than he should be.

'You're an awful scamp, Rowley, and you're not even good-looking enough to excuse it, but we like you', she said.

It was true that Rowley was not much to look at. He had a tolerable figure, but he was of no more than average height, and in clothes he looked thick-set. He had not a single feature that you could call good; he had white teeth, but they were not very even; he had a fresh colour, but not a very clear skin; he had a good head of hair, but it was of a vague brown between dark and fair; his eyes were fairly large, but they were of that pallid blue that is generally described as grey. He had an air of dissipation and people who didn't like him said he looked shifty. It was freely admitted, even by his greatest friends, that he couldn't be trusted. He had a bad record. When he was only just over twenty he had run away and married a girl who was engaged to somebody else, and three years afterwards he had been co-respondent in a divorce case, whereupon his wife divorced him and he had married, not the woman who had been divorced on his account but another, only to leave her two or three years later. He was now just over thirty. He was in short a young man with a shocking reputation which he thoroughly deserved. You would have said there was nothing to recommend him; and Colonel Trail, the travelling Englishman, tall, thin, weatherbeaten, with a lean red face, a grey toothbrush moustache and an air of imbecility, wondered that the Princess had asked him and his wife to meet a damned rotter like that.

'I mean he's not the sort of feller' – he would have said if there'd been anyone to say it to – 'that a decent woman ought to be asked to sit in the same room with.'

He was glad to see, when they took their places at table, that though his wife sat next to Rowley Flint, she was listening to the civil remarks he was making to her with a cold look of disapproval. The worst of it was, the feller wasn't an adventurer or anything like that; in fact, he was a cousin of his wife's; so far as family went he was as good as anybody and he had quite a decent income. The mistake was that he'd never had to earn his living. Oh, well, every family had its black sheep, but what the Colonel couldn't understand was what the women saw in him. He couldn't be expected to know, this simple, honest Englishman, that what Rowley Flint had which explained everything was sex appeal, and the fact that in his relations with women he was unreliable and unscrupulous seemed only to make him more irresistible. However prejudiced she might be against him, he had only to be with a woman for half an hour for her heart to melt, and soon she would be saying to herself that she didn't believe half the things that were said against him. But if she had been asked what it was she saw in him she would have found it hard to answer. He certainly wasn't very good-looking, there was even no distinction in his appearance, he looked like any mechanic in a garage; he wore his smart clothes as if they were overalls, but as if he didn't care a hang what he looked like. It was exasperating that he seemed to be serious about nothing, not even about making love; he made it quite clear that there was only one thing that he wanted from a woman, and his complete lack of sentimentality was intolerably offensive. But there was something that swept you off your feet, a sort of gentleness behind the roughness of his manner, a thrilling warmth behind his mockery, some instinctive understanding of woman as a different creature from man, which was strangely flattering; and the sensuality of his mouth and the caress in his grey eyes. The old Princess had put the matter with her usual crudity:

'Of course he's a bad lot, a thorough wrong 'un, but if I were thirty years younger and he asked me to run away with him I wouldn't hesitate for a moment even though I knew he'd chuck me in a week and I'd be wretched for the rest of my life.'

But the Princess liked general conversation at her table and when her guests were settled down she addressed Mary.

'I'm so sorry Sir Edgar was unable to come tonight.'

'He was sorry, too. He had to go to Cannes.'

The Princess took the rest of the party in.

'It's a great secret, so you mustn't any of you tell anybody, but he's just been made Governor of Bengal.'

'Has he, by Jove!' cried the Colonel. 'A damned nice job to get.'

'Did it come as a surprise?'

'He knew he was one of the people who were being considered', said Mary.

'He'll be the right man in the right place; there's no doubt about that,' said the Colonel. 'If he pulls it off, I shouldn't be surpirsed if later on they didn't make him Viceroy.'

'I can't imagine anything I'd like better than to be Vicereine of India', said the Princess.

'Why don't you marry him on the off-chance?' smiled Mary.

'Oh, isn't he married?' asked Lady Grace.

'No.' The Princess gave Mary a shrewd, malicious look. 'I won't conceal from you that he's been flirting with me outrageously during the six weeks he's been here.'

Rowley chuckled and from beneath his long eyelashes threw a sidelong glance at Mary.

'Have you decided to marry him, Princess? Because if you have, I don't think he's got much chance, poor blighter.'

'I think it would be a very suitable alliance', said Mary.

She knew quite well that both the Princess and Rowley were chaffing her, but she had no intention of giving anything away. Edgar Swift had made it sufficiently plain to his friends and hers in Florence that he was in love with her; and the Princess had more than once tried to find out from her whether anything was going to come of it.

'I don't know whether you'd much like the climate of Calcutta', said Lady Grace, who took everything with complete seriousness.

'Oh, I've reached an age when I prefer my alliances to be temporary', returned the Princess. 'You see, I have no time to waste. That is why I have such a soft spot in my heart for Rowley; his intentions are always dishonourable.'

The Colonel looked at his fish with a frown, which was unreasonable since it consisted of scampi which had arrived from Viareggio that evening, and his wife smiled with constraint.

The restaurant had a small band. Its members were

shabbily dressed in a sort of musical-play Neapolitan costume and they played Neapolitan tunes.

Presently the Princess remarked:

'I think it's about time we had the singer. You'll be astonished. He's really got a magnificent voice, all macaroni and emotion. Harold Atkinson is seriously thinking of having him trained for opera.' She called the head waiter. 'Ask that man to sing that song he sang the other night when I was here.'

'I'm sorry, Excellency, but he's not here to-night. He's sick.'

'How tiresome! I particularly wanted my friends to hear him. I asked them to dine here on purpose for that.'

'He's sent a substitute, but he only plays the violin. I'll tell *him* to play.'

'If there's anything I dislike it's the violin', she answered. 'Why one should want to hear anyone scrape the hairs of a horse's tail against the guts of a dead cat is something I shall never understand.'

The head waiter could speak half a dozen languages fluently, but understood none. He took the Princess's remark to mean that she was pleased with his suggestion, and went up to the violinist, who rose from his chair and stepped forward. He was a dark, slender young man with enormous hungry eyes and a melancholy look. He managed to wear that grotesque costume with a romantic air, but he looked half starved. His smooth face was thin and pinched. He played his piece.

'He's quite frightful, my poor Giovanni', the Princess said to the head waiter.

This time he understood.

'He's not very good, Princess. I'm sorry. I didn't know. But the other will be back to-morrow.'

The band started upon another number and under cover of this Rowley turned to Mary.

'You're looking very beautiful to-night.'

'Thank you.'

His eyes twinkled.

'Shall I tell you one of the things I particularly like about you? Unlike some women, when one tells you you're beautiful, you don't pretend you don't know it. You accept it as naturally as if one told you you had five fingers on each hand.'

'Until I married my looks were my only means of livelihood. When my father died my mother and I had only her pension to live on. If I got parts as soon as I passed out of the Dramatic School it was because I was lucky enough to have the looks I have.'

'I should have thought you could have made a fortune on the movies.'

She laughed.

'Unfortunately I had absolutely no talent. Nothing but looks. Perhaps in time I might have learnt to act, but I married and left the stage.'

A faint shadow seemed to fall on her face and she looked for a moment disconsolately into her past. Rowley looked at her perfect profile. She was indeed a beautiful creature. It was not only that she had exquisite features; what made her so remarkable was her wonderful colouring.

'You're a brown and gold girl, aren't you?' he said.

Her hair was of a dark rich gold, her large eyes deep brown, and her skin pale gold. It was her colouring which took away the coldness which her regular features might have given her face and gave her a warmth and a richness which were infinitely alluring.

'I think you're the most beautiful woman I've ever seen.'

'And how many women have you said that to?'

'A good many. But that doesn't make it any less true when I say it now.'

She laughed.

'I suppose it doesn't. But we'll leave it at that, shall we?'

'Why? It's a subject that I find excessively interesting.'

'People have been telling me I was beautiful since I was sixteen and it's ceased to excite me very much. It's an asset and I should be a fool not to know its value. It has its disadvantages as well.'

'You're a very sensible girl.'

'Now you're paying me a compliment that does flatter me.'

'I wasn't trying to flatter you.'

'Weren't you? It sounded to me like an opening I've heard very often before. Give a plain woman a hat and a pretty one a book. Isn't that the idea?'

He was not in the least disconcerted.

'Aren't you a trifle caustic to-night?'

'I'm sorry you should think that. I merely wanted to make it quite plain once and for all that there's nothing doing.'

'Don't you know that I'm desperately in love with you?'

'Desperately is perhaps hardly the word. You've made it pretty clear during the last few weeks that you'd be glad to have a little flutter with me. A widow, pretty and unattached, in a place like Florence – it looked just your mark.'

'Can you blame me? Surely it's very natural that in spring a young man's fancy should lightly turn to thoughts of love.'

His manner was so disarming, his frankness so engaging that Mary could not but smile.

'I'm not blaming you. Only so far as I'm concerned, you're barking up the wrong tree and I hate the idea of you wasting your time.'

'Full of consideration, aren't you? In point of fact I have plenty of time to waste.'

'Ever since I was sixteen men have been making love to me. Whatever they are, old or young, ugly or handsome, they seem to think you're there for no purpose except to gratify their lust.'

'Have you never been in love?'

'Yes, once.'

'Who with?'

'My husband. That's why I married him.'

There was a moment's pause. The Princess broke in with some casual remark and once more the conversation became general.

3

They had dined late and soon after eleven the Princess called for her bill. When it grew evident that they were about to go, the violinist who had played to them came forward with a plate. There were a few coins on it from diners at other tables and some small notes. What they thus received was the band's only remuneration. Mary opened her bag.

'Don't bother', said Rowley. 'I'll give him a trifle.'

He took a ten-lira note out of his pocket and put it on the plate.

'I'd like to give him something too', said Mary. She laid a hundred-lira note on the others. The man looked surprised, gave Mary a searching look, bowed slightly and withdrew.

'What on earth did you give him that for?' exclaimed Rowley. 'That's absurd.'

'He plays so badly and he looks so wretched.'

'But they don't expect anything like that.'

'I know. That's why I gave it. It'll mean so much to him. It may make all the difference to his life.'

The Italian members of the party drove off in their respective cars and the Princess took the Trails in hers.

'You might drop Rowley at his hotel, Mary', she said. 'He's right out of my way.'

'Would you mind?' he asked.

Mary had a suspicion that this plan had been arranged beforehand, for she knew how the lewd old woman loved to forward love affairs and Rowley was a favourite of hers, but there seemed no possibility of refusing so reasonable a request and so she answered that of course she would be delighted. They got into her car and drove along the quay. The full moon flooded their way with radiance. They spoke little. Rowley had a feeling that she was occupied with thoughts in which he had no part and he did not wish to disturb them. But when they came to his hotel he said:

'It's such a gorgeous night; it seems a pity to waste it by going to bed: wouldn't you drive on a little? You're not sleepy, are you?'

'No.'

'Let's drive into the country.'

'Isn't it rather late for that?'

'Are you afraid of the country or afraid of me?'

'Neither.'

She drove on. She followed the course of the river, and presently they were going through fields with only a cottage here and there by the roadside or, a little way back, a white farm-house with tall cypresses that stood black and solemn against the moonlight.

'Are you going to marry Edgar Swift?' he asked suddenly.

She looked round at him.

'Did you know I was thinking of him?'

'How should I?'

She paused for a while before she answered.

'Before he went away to-day he asked me to. I said I'd give him an answer when he got back.'

'You're not in love with him then?'

Mary slowed up. It looked as though she wanted to talk.

'What makes you think that?'

'If you had been you wouldn't have wanted three days to think it over. You'd have said yes there and then.'

'I suppose that's true. No, I'm not in love with him.'

'He's in love with you all right.'

'He was a friend of my father's and I've known him all my life. He was wonderfully kind to me when I wanted kindness, and I'm grateful to him.'

'He must be twenty years older than you.'

'Twenty-four.'

'Are you dazzled by the position he can give you?'

'I dare say. Don't you think most women would be? After all, I'm not inhuman.'

'Do you think it would be much fun to live with a man you weren't in love with?'

'But I don't want love. I'm fed to the teeth with love.'

She said this so violently that Rowley was startled.

'That's a strange thing to say at your age.'

They were well out in the country now, on a narrow road; the full moon shone down from an unclouded sky. She stopped the car.

'You see, I was madly in love with my husband. They told me I was a fool to marry him; they said he was a gambler and a drunkard; I didn't care. He wanted me to marry him so much. He had plenty of money then, but I'd have married him if he hadn't had a cent. You don't know how charming he was in those days, so good to look at, so gay and light-hearted. The fun we used to have together! He had immense vitality. He was so kind and gentle and sweet – when he was sober. When he was drunk he was noisy and boastful and vulgar and quarrelsome. It was terribly distressing; I used to be so ashamed. I couldn't be angry with him; he was so sorry afterwards; he didn't want to drink; when he was alone with me he was as sober as anyone, it was only when there were other people there that he got excited, and after two or three drinks there was no holding him; then I used to wait till he was so blas that he let me lead him away and at last I could put him to bed. I did everything I knew to cure him, it was useless; it's no good. I don't believe a drunk can ever be cured. And I was forced into the position of nurse and keeper. It irritated him beyond endurance when I tried to restrain him, but what else could I do? It was so difficult, I didn't want him to look upon me as a sort of governess, but I had to do what I could to keep him from drinking. Sometimes I couldn't help flying into a passion with him and then we'd have an awful row. You see, he was a dreadful gambler and when he was drunk he'd lose hundreds of pounds. If he hadn't died when he did he'd have gone bankrupt and

I should have had to go back to the stage to keep him. As it is I have a few hundreds a year and the bits and pieces of jewellery he gave me when we were first married. Sometimes he wouldn't come back all night and then I knew he'd got blind and picked up the first woman he met. At first I used to be furiously jealous and unhappy, but at last I got to prefer it, for if he didn't do that he'd come home and make love to me with his breath stinking of whisky, all hunched up, his face distorted, and I knew it wasn't love that made him passionate but drink, just drink. I or another woman, it made no difference, and his kisses made me sick and his desire horrified and mortified me. And when he'd satisfied his lust he'd sink into the snoring sleep of drunkenness. You're surprised that I should say I was fed to the teeth with love. For years I only knew the humiliation of it.'

'But why didn't you leave him?'

'How could I leave him? He was so dependent on me. When anything went wrong, if he got into trouble, if he was ill, it was me he came to for help. He clung to me like a child.' Her voice broke. 'He was so broken then that my heart bled for him. Though he was unfaithful to me, though he hid himself from me so that he could drink without restraint, though I exasperated him sometimes so that he hated me, deep down he always loved me, he knew I'd never let him down and he knew that except for me he'd go all to pieces. He was so beastly when he was drunk he had no friends, only the riff-raff that sponged on him and bled him and robbed him; he knew I was the only person in the world who cared if he lived or died and I knew that I was the only person who stood between him and absolute ruin. And when he died, in my arms, I was broken-hearted.'

The tears were flowing down Mary's face and she made no effort to restrain them. Rowley, thinking perhaps that it would relieve her to cry, sat still and said no word. Presently he lit a cigarette.

'Give me one too. I'm being stupid.'

He took a cigarette out of his case and handed it to her.

'I'd like my handkerchief. It's in my bag.'

The bag was between them and when he opened it to find her handkerchief he was surprised to feel a revolver.

'What have you got a gun here for?'

'Edgar didn't like the idea of my driving about alone. He made me promise to take it. I know it's idiotic.' But the new subject that Rowley had brought up helped her to regain her self-control. 'I'm sorry to have got so emotional.'

'When did your husband die?'

'A year ago. And now I'm thankful he died. I know now that my life was wretched with him and he had nothing to look forward to but hopeless misery.'

'He was young to die, wasn't he?'

'He was smashed up in a motor accident. He was drunk. He was driving at sixty miles an hour and skidded on a slippery road. He died in a few hours. Mercifully I was able to get to him. His last words were: "I've always loved you, Mary".' She sighed. 'His death has given us both freedom.'

For a little while they sat and smoked in silence. Rowley lit another cigarette on the stub of the first.

'Are you sure you're not committing yourself to a slavery just as great when you marry a man who means nothing to you?' he asked, as though their conversation had gone on without interruption.

'How well do you know Edgar?'

'I've met him fairly often during the five or six weeks he's been here dangling at your skirts. He's the Empire-builder; it's not a type that has ever very much appealed to me.'

Mary giggled.

'No, I should hardly think it would. He's strong, he's clever, he's trustworthy.'

'Everything I'm not, in short.'

'Can't we leave you out of it for the minute?'

'All right. Go on with his virtues.'

'He's kind and considerate. He's ambitious. He's a man who has done great things and he'll do still greater in future. It may be I can help him. I can't hope that you'll think it anything but idiotic when I tell you that I should like to be of some use in the world.'

'You haven't got a very good opinion of me, have you?'

'No, I haven't', chuckled Mary.

'I wonder why.'

'If you'd like to know I'll tell you', she answered coolly. 'Because you're a waster and a rotter. Because you think of nothing but having a good time and as many women as are fools enough to fall for you.'

'I look upon that as a very accurate description. I was lucky enough to inherit an income which made it unnecessary for me to earn my living. Do you think I should have got some job that would have taken the bread out of the mouth of a poor devil who needed it? So far as I know I've only got this one life to dispose of. I like it awfully. I'm in the fortunate position of being able to live for living's sake. What a fool I should be if I didn't make the most of my opportunities! I like women, and strangely enough they like me. I'm young and I know youth doesn't last for ever. Why shouldn't I have as good a time as I can while I have the chance?'

'It would be hard to find a greater contrast to Edgar.'

'I agree. It may be that I'd be easier to live with. I should certainly be more fun.'

'You forget that Edgar wishes to marry me. You are suggesting a much more temporary arrangement.'

'What makes you think that?'

'Well, for one thing, you happen to be married already.'

'That's where you're mistaken. I was divorced a couple of months ago.'

'You kept very quiet about it.'

'Naturally. Women have funny ideas about marriage. It makes things easier all round if there's never any question of that. We all know where we are then.'

'I see your point', smiled Mary. 'Why should you divulge this guilty secret to me? With the idea that if I behaved myself and gave satisfaction you might in due course reward me with a wedding ring?'

'Darling, I'm quite intelligent enough to know you're no fool.'

'You need not call me darling.'

'Damn it all, I'm in process of making you a proposal of marriage.'

'Are you? Why?'

'I don't think it's a bad idea. Do you?'

'Rotten. What on earth put it in your head?'

'It just occurred to me. You see, when you told me about your husband I suddenly realised that I was terribly fond of you. That's different from being in love, you know, but I'm in love too. I feel a great tenderness towards you.'

'I'd rather you didn't say things like that. You are a devil, you seem to know instinctively what to say that'll melt a woman.'

'I couldn't say them if I didn't feel them.'

'Oh, shut up. It's lucky for you that I have a cool head and a sense of humour. Let's go back to Florence. I'll drop you at your hotel.'

'Does that mean the answer is no?'

'It does.'

'Why?'

'I'm sure it'll surprise you; I'm not in the least in love with you.'

'It doesn't surprise me. I knew it; but you would be if you gave yourself half a chance.'

'Modest fellow, aren't you? But I don't want to give myself half a chance.'

'Are you determined to marry Edgar Swift?'

'Now I am, yes. Thank you for letting me talk to you. It was hard having no one I could talk to. You've helped me to make up my mind.'

'I'm damned if I see how.'

'Women don't reason in the same way that men do. All you've said, all I've said, the recollection of the life with my husband, the misery, the mortification – well, against that Edgar stands like a great rock; he's so strong and so staunch. I know I can rely on him; he'd never let me down, because he couldn't. He offers me security. I have so great an affection for him at this moment that it's almost love.'

'It's rather a narrow road', said Rowley; 'would you like me to turn the car for you?'

'I'm perfectly capable of turning my own car, thank you', she answered.

His remark had given her a moment's irritation, not because it reflected on her driving, but because for some reason it made what she had just said seem a trifle high-flown. He chuckled.

'There's a ditch on one side and a ditch on the other. I shall be vexed if you pitch me into either one or the other.'

'Hold your bloody tongue', she said.

He lit a cigarette and watched her as she advanced, turned the wheel with an effort of all her strength, stopped the engine and started it again, put the clutch in reverse and gingerly backed, grew very hot, and eventually got the car round and set off on the homeward journey. They drove in silence till they reached the hotel. It was late now and the door was shut. Rowley made no attempt to get out.

'Here we are', said Mary.

'I know.'

He sat silent for a moment or two staring straight in front of him. She gave him a questioning look and with a smile he turned to her.

'You're a fool, Mary my dear. Oh, I know, you've turned me down. That's all right. Though I dare say I'd have made a better husband than you think. But you're a fool to marry a man twenty-five years older than yourself. How old are you? Thirty at the outside. You're not a fish. One only has to look at your mouth and the warmth of your eyes, and at the lines of your body, to know that you're a passionate and sensual woman. Oh, I know you had a rotten break. But at your age one recovers from those things; you'll fall in love again. D'you think you can ignore your sexual instincts? That beautiful body of yours is made for love; it won't allow you to deny it. You're too young to shut the door on life.'

'You disgust me, Rowley. You talk as though bed were its aim and end.'

'Have you never had a lover?'

'Never.'

'Many men besides your husband must have loved you.'

'I don't know. Some have said they did. You can't think how little they meant to me. I can't say I've resisted temptation; I've never been tempted.'

'Oh, how can you waste your youth and beauty?

They last so short a time. What's the good of riches if one does nothing with them? You're a kind woman and a generous one. Haven't you ever the desire to give of your riches?'

Mary was silent for an instant.

'Shall I tell you something? I'm afraid you'll think me even more foolish than you do.'

'Very possibly. But tell me all the same.'

'I should be a fool if I didn't know I was prettier than most women. It's true that sometimes I felt that I had something to give that might mean a great deal to the person I gave it to. Does that sound frightfully conceited?'

'No. It's the plain truth.'

'I've had a lot of time to myself lately and I dare say I've wasted too much of it on idle thoughts. If ever I'd taken a lover it wouldn't have been a man like you. My poor Rowley, you're the last man I would ever have had an affair with. But I've sometimes thought that if I ever ran across someone who was poor, alone and unhappy, who'd never had any pleasure in life, who'd never known any of the good things money can buy – and if I could give him a unique experience, an hour of absolute happiness, something that he'd never dreamt of and that would never be repeated, then I'd give him gladly everything I had to give.'

'I never heard such a crazy idea in my life!' cried Rowley.

'Well, now you know', she answered brightly. 'So get out and let me drive home.'

'Will you be all right alone?'

'Of course.'

'Then good night. Marry your Empire-builder and be damned to you.'

4

Mary drove through the silent streets of Florence, along the road by which she had come, and then up the hill on the top of which was the villa. The hill was steep and wound sharply with horse-shoe turns. About half-way up was a little semi-circular terrace, with a tall, very old cypress and a parapet in front, from which one got a view of the Cathedral and the towers of Florence. Tempted by the beauty of the night Mary stopped the car and got out. She walked to the edge and looked over. The sight that met her eyes, the valley flooded with the full moon under the vastness of the cloudless sky, was so lovely that it wrung her heart with a throb of pain.

Suddenly she was aware that a man was standing in the shadow of the cypress. She saw the gleam of his cigarette. He came towards her. She was a trifle startled, but had no intention of showing it. He took off his hat.

'Excuse me, are you not the lady who was so generous in the restaurant?' he said. 'I should like to thank you.'

She recognised him.

'You are the violinist.'

He no longer wore that absurd Neapolitan costume, but nondescript clothes which looked threadbare and dingy. He spoke English well enough but with a foreign accent.

'I owed my landlady for my board and lodging. The people I live with are very good to me, but they are poor and they need the money. Now I shall be able to pay them.'

'What are you doing here?' asked Mary.

'It is on my way home. I stopped to look at the view.

'Do you live near here then?'

'I live in one of the cottages just before you come to your villa.'

'How do you know where I live?'

'I've seen you passing in your car. I know that you have a beautiful garden and there are frescoes in the villa.'

'Have you been in it?'

'No. How should I? The contadini have told me about it.'

Mary had lost the slight nervousness which she had had for a moment. He was a pleasant-spoken, rather shy young man; she remembered how ill at ease he had looked in the restaurant.

'Would you like to come and see the garden and the frescoes?' she said.

'It would give me much pleasure. When would it be convenient?'

Rowley and his unexpected proposal of marriage had amused and excited her. She had no wish to go to bed.

'Why not now?' she said on an impulse.

'Now?' he repeated, surprised.

'Why not? The garden is never so beautiful as under the full moon.'

'I should be very pleased', he said primly.

'Jump into the car. I'll drive you up.'

He took his seat by her side. She continued on her way and they came to a group of cottages huddled together.

'That is where I live', he told her.

She slowed down and looked reflectively at the poverty-stricken little houses. They were horribly sordid. She drove on and presently they came to the gates of her villa. They stood open and she drove in.

She parked the car and they walked up the narrow drive. The principal rooms and Mary's bedroom were on the second floor to which you ascended by a fine flight of steps. She opened the door and turned on the lights. There was nothing much to see in the hall and she took the young man straight into the drawing-room with the painted walls. It was a noble apartment and the owners of the villa had furnished it with period pieces of fine quality. Flowers arranged in great vases mitigated its stately severity. The frescoes were somewhat damaged and had been none too well restored, but with all those figures in their sixteenth-century clothes they gave an impression of a multifarious and magnificent vitality.

'Wonderful, wonderful!' he cried. 'I didn't think one ever saw such things except in a museum. I never realised that people could possess them.'

It gave her a thrill to see his delight. She did not

think it necessary to tell him that there was not a chair in which you could sit with comfort nor that, with those marble floors and that vaulted ceiling, except in the warmest of warm weather you shivered with cold.

'And is it all yours?' he asked.

'Oh, no. It belongs to friends of mine. They've lent it to me while they're away.'

'I'm sorry. You are beautiful and it's right that you should possess beautiful things.'

'Come along', she said, 'and I'll get you a glass of wine and then we'll go and look at the garden.'

'No, I had no dinner. Wine would go to my head.'

'Why did you have no dinner?'

He gave a careless, boyish laugh.

'I had no money. But never mind about that; I shall eat to-morrow.'

'Oh, but that's awful. Come into the kitchen and we'll see if we can't find something for you to eat now.'

'I'm not hungry. This is better than food. Let me see the garden with the moon shining.'

'The garden will keep and so will the moon. I'm going to make you some supper and then you shall see anything you like.'

They went down into the kitchen. It was vast, with a stone floor and a huge old-fashioned range where you might have cooked for fifty people. Nina and Ciro were long since in bed and asleep and the cook had gone home to her cottage halfway down the hill. Mary and the stranger, hunting about for food, felt like a pair of burglars. They found bread and wine, eggs, bacon and butter. Mary turned on the electric stove which the Leonards had put in, started to toast some slices of bread and broke the eggs into a frying-pan to scramble them.

'Cut some rashers of bacon', she told the young man, 'and we'll fry them. What is your name?'

With the bacon in one hand and a knife in the other, he clicked his heels together.

'Karl Richter, student of art.'

'Oh, I thought you were Italian', she said lightly, as she beat the eggs. 'That sounds German.'

'I was Austrian when Austria existed.'

There was a sullenness in his tone which made Mary give him a questioning look.

'How is it you speak English? Have you ever been to England?'

'No. I learnt it at school and at the University.' Suddenly he smiled. 'You're marvellous to be able to do that.'

'To do what?'

'Cook.'

'Would it surprise you if I told you I'd been a working girl and not only was able to cook for myself, but had to?'

'I shouldn't believe it.'

'Would you rather believe that I'd lived in luxury all my life with a host of servants to look after me?'

'Yes. Like a princess in a fairy story.'

'Then it's true. I can scramble eggs and fry bacon

because that was one of the gifts I received at my christening from my fairy godmother.'

When everything was ready they put it on a tray and, Mary leading, went into the dining-room. It was a large room with a painted ceiling, with a tapesty at each end and great gilt-wood sconces on the side walls. They sat opposite one another in tall stately chairs at a refectory table.

'I'm ashamed of my poor and shabby clothes', he smiled. 'In this splendid room I should be dressed in silk and fine velvet like the cavaliers in an old picture.'

His suit was shabby, his shoes patched and his shirt, open at the neck, frayed. He wore no tie. By the light of the tall candles on the table his eyes were dark and cavernous. He had a strange head with close-cropped black hair, high cheek-bones, hollow cheeks, a pallid skin and a look of strain which was somewhat moving. It occurred to Mary that in costume, dressed, say, like one of those young princes in a picture by Bronzino at the Uffizi, he would have been very nearly beautiful.

'How old are you?' she asked him.

'Twenty-three.'

'What else matters?'

'What is the good of youth that has no opportunity? I live in a prison and there's no escape from it.'

'Are you an artist?'

He laughed.

'Can you ask me after hearing me play? I'm not a violinist. When I escaped from Austria I got work in a hotel, but business was bad and I was sent away. I've had one or two odd jobs, but it's difficult to get them when you're a foreigner and your papers aren't in order. I play the fiddle when I get the chance just to keep body and soul together, but I don't get the chance every day.'

'Why did you have to leave Austria?'

'Some of us students protested against the Anschluss. We tried to organize resistance. It was stupid of course. We hadn't a hope. The only result was that two of us were shot and the rest put in a concentration camp. They put me in for six months, but I escaped and crossed the mountains into Italy.'

'It all sounds rather horrible', said Mary.

It was a lame and inadequate thing to say, but it was all she could think of. He gave her an ironical smile.

'I'm not the only one, you know. There are thousands and thousands of us in the world now. Anyhow I'm free.'

'But what are your plans for the future?'

A look of despair crossed his face and he was about to answer. But he made an impatient gesture and laughed.

'Don't let me think of that now. Let me enjoy this priceless moment. Nothing has ever happened to me like this in all my life. I want to enjoy it so that whatever comes to me later it will be a recollection that I can always treasure.'

Mary looked at him strangely and it seemed to her that she could hear the beating of her heart. It had been almost a joke what she had said to Rowley, the reverie of an idle day that, when the moment came, she knew she would shrink from. Had the moment come now? She felt queerly reckless. She drank very little as a rule and the strong red wine she had been drinking to keep him company had gone to her head. There was something mysteriously disturbing in thus sitting in that vast room with its memories of long ago opposite this young man with the tragic face. It was long past midnight. The air that came in through the open windows was warm and scented. Mary felt a sort of languor running through her excitement; her heart seemed to melt in her bosom and at the same time the blood seemed to race madly through her veins. She rose abruptly from the table.

'Now I will show you the garden and then you must go.'

Access to it was most convenient from the great room in which were the frescoes, and thither she led him. On the way through he paused to look at a handsome cassone that stood against the wall; then he caught sight of the gramophone.

'How strange that looks in these surroundings!'

'I sometimes put it on when I'm sitting in the garden by myself.'

'May I put it on now?'

'If you like.'

He turned the switch. By chance the record was that of a Strauss waltz. He gave a little cry of delight.

'Vienna. It's one of our dear Viennese waltzes.'

He looked at her with shining eyes. His face was

transfigured. She had an intuition of what he wanted to ask her, and saw at the same time that he was too timid to speak. She smiled.

'Can you dance?'

'Oh, yes; I can do that. I dance better than I play.'

'Let me see.'

He put his arm round her and in that sumptuous, empty room, in the dead of night, they waltzed to the old-fashioned charming tune of the Viennese conductor. Then she took his hand and led him out into the garden. By the garish light of day it had sometimes a look that was a trifle forlorn, like a woman much loved who has lost her loveliness; but now under the full moon, with its trimmed hedges and ancient trees, with its grotto and its lawns, it was thrilling and secret. The centuries fell away and wandering there you felt yourself the inhabitant of a fresher, younger world in which instinct was more reckless and consequences less material. The light summer air was scented with the white flowers of night.

They walked silently, hand in hand.

'It's so beautiful', he murmured at last, 'it's almost unbearable.' He quoted that celebrated line of Goethe's in which Faust, satisfied at length, begs the fleeting moment to stay. 'You must be very happy here.'

'Very', she smiled.

'I'm glad. You're kind and good and generous. You deserve happiness. I should like to think that you have everything in the world you desire.'

She chuckled.

'At all events I have everything I have any right to hope for.'

He sighed.

'I should like to die this night. Nothing so wonderful will ever happen to me again. I shall think of it all my life. I shall always have this evening to remember, the glimpse of your beauty and the recollection of this lovely spot. I shall always think of you as a goddess in heaven and I shall pray to you as though you were the Madonna.'

He lifted her hand to his lips and with an awkward, touching little bow, kissed it. She gently touched his face. Suddenly he fell on his knees and kissed the hem of her dress. Then a great exaltation seized her. She took his head in her hands, raising him towards her, and kissed his eyes and his mouth. There was something solemn and mystical in the action. She had a feeling that was strange to her. Her heart was filled with loving kindness.

He rose to his feet and passionately clasped her in his arms. He was twenty-three. She was not a goddess to pray to, but a woman to possess.

They went back into the silent house.

5

It was dark in the room, but the windows were wide open and the moon shone in. Mary was sitting in a straight-backed antique chair and the youth sat at her feet leaning his head against her knees. He was smoking a cigarette and in the darkness the glow shone red. In answer to her questioning he told her that his father had been head of the police in one of the smaller towns of Austria during the Dollfuss Government and he had put down with severity the various agitations which disturbed the peace during those troubled times. When Schuschnigg became head of the State after the assassination of the little peasant chancellor, his firmness and determined attitude had maintained him in his post. He favoured the restoration of the Archduke Otto because he thought that this was the only way to prevent Austria, which he loved with ardent patriotism, from being absorbed by Germany. During the three years that followed he aroused the bitter enmity of the Austrian Nazis by the stern measures he took to curb their treasonable activities. On that fatal day when the German troops marched into the defenceless little country he shot himself through the heart. The young Karl, his boy, was then finishing his education. He had specialised in the history of art, but was going to be a schoolmaster. At the moment nothing could be done, and with rage in his heart he listened among the crowd to the speech Hitler made at Linz from the balcony of the Landhaus when he entered the town in triumph. He heard the Austrians shout themselves hoarse with joy as they acclaimed their conqueror. But this enthusiasm was soon followed by disillusion, and when some of the bolder spirits gathered together to form a secret association to fight the alien rule by every means in their power they found many adherents. Karl was among them. They held meetings which they were convinced were private; they conspired in an ineffective way; they were no more than boys any of them, and they never dreamt that every move they made, every word they said, was reported at the headquarters of the secret police. One day they were all arrested. Two were shot as a warning to the rest, and the others were sent to a concentration camp. Karl escaped after three months and by good luck was able to get over the frontier into the Italian Tyrol. He had no passport nor papers of any kind, for these had been taken from him in the concentration camp, and he lived in terror of being arrested and either put in prison as a vagabond or deported back to the Reich, where a harsh punishment awaited him.

'If I'd only had enough money to buy a revolver I'd have shot myself as my father did.'

He took her hand and placed it on his chest.

'There, between the fourth and fifth ribs. Just where your fingers are.'

'Don't say such things', said Mary, with a shudder, snatching her hand away.

He gave a mirthless laugh.

'You don't know how often I've looked at the Arno and wondered when the time would come when nothing was left to me but to throw myself in.'

Mary sighed deeply. His fate seemed so cruel that any words she might have found to console him could only have been futile. He pressed her hand.

'Don't sigh', he said tenderly. 'I regret nothing any more. It's all been worth it for this wonderful night.'

They ceased to speak. Mary thought of his miserably story. There was no way out. What could *she* do? Give him money? That would help him for a little while perhaps, but that was all; he was a romantic creature, his high-flown, extravagant language was that of a boy who knew more of books than, for all his terrible experiences, of life, and it was quite possible that he would refuse to take anything from her. On a sudden a cock crew. The sound broke the silence of the night so shrilly that she was startled. She took her hand away from his.

'You must go now, my dear', she said.

'Not yet', he cried. 'Not yet, my love.'

'The dawn will break soon.'

'Not for a long time yet.' He raised himself to his knees and threw his arms round her. 'I adore you.'

She disengaged herself.

'No, really you must go. It's so late. Please.'

She felt rather than saw the sweet smile that broke on his lips. He scrambled to his feet. He looked for his coat and shoes and she switched on a light. When he was once more dressed he took her in his arms again.

'My lovely one', he whispered. 'You've made me so happy.'

'I'm glad.'

'You've given me something to live for. Now I have you I have everything. Let the future look after itself. Life's not so bad; something will turn up.'

'You'll never forget?'

'Never.'

She lifted her lips to his.

'Good-bye then.'

'Good-bye till when?' he murmured passionately.

She freed herself again.

'Good-bye for ever, my dear. I'm leaving here very soon – in three or four days, I expect.' It seemed difficult to say what she had to say. 'We can't see one another any more. You see, I'm not free.'

'Are you married? They told me you were a widow.'

It would have been easy to lie. She did not know what prevented her. She hedged.

'What did you think I meant when I said I wasn't free? I tell you it's impossible we should ever meet again. You don't want to ruin my life, do you?'

'But I must see you again. Once more, only once more. Or else I shall die.'

'My dear, don't be unreasonable. I tell you it's impossible. When we part now we part for ever.'

'But I love you. Don't you love me?'

She hesitated a moment. She did not want to be

unkind, but thought it necessary at that moment to tell the plain truth. She shook her head and smiled a little.

'No.'

He stared at her as if he didn't understand.

'Then why did you take me?'

'You were lonely and miserable. I wanted to give you a few moments' happiness.'

'Oh, how cruel! How monstrously cruel!'

Her voice broke.

'Don't say that. I didn't mean to be cruel. My heart was full of tenderness and pity.'

'I never asked for your pity. Why didn't you leave me alone? You have shown me heaven and now you want to thrust me back to earth. No. No. No.'

He seemed to grow in stature as he flung the words at her. There was something tragic in his indignation. She was vaguely impressed. It had never occurred to her that he would take it like that.

'Perhaps I've been very stupid', she said. 'I didn't want to hurt you.'

There was no love in his eyes now but cold, sullen anger. His white face had gone whiter still and it was like a death mask. It made her uneasy. She knew now what a fool she'd been. The servants slept far away and if she screamed they would not hear her. Idiot, idiot that she was! The only thing was to keep her head and not show him that she was frightened.

'I'm terribly sorry', she faltered. 'I didn't mean to hurt your feelings. If there's anything I can do to make up I'll only be too glad to do it.'

He frowned darkly.

'What are you doing now? Are you offering me money? I don't want your money. How much money have you got here?'

She took her bag which was on the dressing-table, and as she put her hand in felt the revolver. It gave her a start. She had never fired one in her life. Oh, it was nonsense to suppose it would come to that. But thank God she had it. Dear Edgar, he hadn't been such an old donkey after all. The inconsequent thought flashed through her mind that it was not with the idea of her ever finding herself in such a situation that he had forced it on her. Even at that moment the idea amused her and she regained her self-possession.

'I've got two or three thousand lire. It would be enough to get you into Switzerland. You'd be safer there. Believe me, I shan't miss it.'

'Of course you won't miss it. You're rich, aren't you? You're rich enough to pay for the pleasure of a night's fun. D'you always have to pay for your lovers? If I wanted money d'you think I'd be satisfied with a few lire? I should take the pearls you wore, and the bracelets you had on your arm.'

'You can have them, too, if you want them. They mean nothing to me. They're on the dressing-table. Take them.'

'You vile woman. Are you so vile that you think any man can be bought off at a price? You fool, if money had meant so much to me don't you think I could have made terms with the Nazis? I didn't need to be an outcast. I didn't need to starve.'

'My God, why can't I make you understand? I meant to do you a kindness, you seem to think I've done you harm. I want to make up for the harm. If I've offended you, if I've hurt you, I ask your forgiveness. I only wanted your good.'

'You lie. An idle, sensual, worthless woman. What good have you ever done in your life, I wonder? You go about seeking excitement, new experiences, anything to cheat your boredom, and you don't care what injury you cause to others. But this time you've made a mistake. It's a risk to take strange men into one's house. I took you for a goddess and you're just a whore. It would be a good thing, maybe, if I strangled you to prevent you from hurting others as you've hurt me. I could, you know. Who would ever suspect me? Who saw me come into this house?'

He took a step towards her. She was seized with panic. He looked sinister and menacing. His gaunt face was distorted with hatred and those dark deep-set eyes flashed. She made an effort at self-control. She was still holding the bag in her hand; she snatched the revolver and pointed it at him.

'If you don't go at once I shall fire!' she cried.

'Fire then.'

He took another step towards her.

'If you come an inch nearer I shall shoot.'

'Shoot. Do you think life means anything to me? You will be robbing me of an intolerable burden.

Shoot. Shoot and I'll forgive you everything. I love you!'

His face was transfigured. The sullen rage was wiped clean off it and his great black eyes shone with exaltation. He came towards her, his head thrown back, his arms outspread, offering his breast to her aim.

'You can say a thief broke into your room and you shot him dead. Quick, quick.'

She let the revolver fall from her hand and throwing herself into a chair hid her face and burst into a passion of tears. He looked at her for a moment.

'Hadn't you the courage? Poor child. How stupid you are, how terribly stupid. You mustn't play with men as you played with me. Come.'

He put his arms round her and tried to lift her to her feet. She did not know what he wanted and, still sobbing bitterly, clung to the chair. He hit her hand roughly, so that, crying out with the pain, she let go instinctively; with a swift gesture he picked her up, carried her across the room and roughly threw her down on the bed. He flung himself beside her, took her in his arms and covered her face with kisses. She tried to get away from him, but he would not let her go. He was strong, much stronger than he looked, and she was powerless in his firm grasp. At last she ceased to resist.

A few minutes later he got up. She was shattered. He stood at the side of the bed looking down at her.

'You asked me not to forget you. I shall forget, but you won't.'

She did not stir. She glared at him with terrified eyes. He gave a little harsh laugh.

'Don't be afraid. I'm not going to hurt you.'

She said nothing. Unable to withstand the anger of his cruel stare, she closed her eyes. She heard him move stealthily about the darkened room. Suddenly she heard a report and then the sound of a fall. It brought her to her feet with a shriek of dismay.

'God, what have you done?'

He was lying in front of the window, with the moonlight pouring down on him. She flung herself down on her knees beside him and called him by his name.

'Karl, Karl, what have you done?'

She took him by the hand and when she dropped it, it fell with a lifeless thud on the floor. She put her hand on his face and on his heart. He was dead. She fell back on her heels and stared at the body with terror. Her mind went blank. She did not know what to do. Her head swam and she was afraid she was going to faint.

Suddenly she started, for she had heard a pattering in the passage, the patter of bare feet; then it stopped and she knew that there was someone outside the door, listening. She stared at it in a panic. There was a soft little knock. She was trembling violently, and it was only by a violent effort that she choked down the scream that came to her lips. She sat there, on the floor, as still as the dead man by her side. The knock was repeated. She forced herself to speak.

'Yes, what is it?'

'Are you all right, Signora?' It was Nina's voice. 'I thought I heard a bang.'

Mary, clenching her hands, dug her nails into her palms in order to force herself to speak naturally.

'You must have been dreaming. I heard nothing. Go to bed.'

'Very well, Signora.'

There was a moment's pause, and then she heard the bare feet pattering away again. As though she could follow the sound with her eyes Mary, turning her head, followed it down the passage. She had spoken instinctively to give herself time to gather her wits together. She sighed deeply. But something had to be done. She leant over to look once more at the Austrian. She shuddered. Getting on to her feet again, she put her hands under the dead man's arms and tried to drag him out of the window. She hardly knew what she was doing; it was some blind impulse that led her to want somehow to get him out of the room. But the body was heavy. She gave a gasp of anguish; she felt as weak as a rat. Now she couldn't think what to do. Suddenly it occurred to her that it had been madness to send Nina away. How could she explain that, with that man lying dead in the room, she had said there was nothing the matter? Why had she said that she had heard no sound when he had shot himself within those four walls? A confused rush of all the terrible difficulties of her position swirled in her head like a whirlpool. And the shame. The dishonour. And what answer could she give when they asked her why he had killed himself? The only thing she could do was to tell the truth; and the truth was vile. It was awful to be alone there without anyone to help her and tell her what to do. In her distraction she felt she must see someone. Help, help, she must have help. Rowley. He was the only person she could think of. She was sure he would come if she asked him. He liked her, he said he loved her, and bad lot as he was, he was a good sort; at all events he'd give her advice. But it was so late. How could she expect to get hold of him like that, in the middle of the night? But she couldn't wait till daybreak, nothing would be any good unless it were done at once.

There was a phone by her bed. She knew the number because Edgar had stayed at the same hotel and she had often called him. She dialled it. At first there was no reply and then an Italian voice answered. Presumably it was a night porter whom she had roused out of a stolen nap. She asked to be put through to Rowley's room. She could hear the bell ringing, but there was no answer. For a moment she was terrified, thinking that he was out; he might have gone somewhere after he left her, to gamble or, being what he was, he might have found some woman and gone home with her. She gave a sigh of relief when she heard a cross, sleepy voice.

'Yes. What is it?'

'Rowley. It's me. Mary. I'm in frightful trouble.'

She suddenly felt that he was wide awake. He gave a little chuckle.

'Late to get into trouble, isn't it? What's it all about?'

'I can't tell you. It's serious. I want you to come here.'

'When?'

'Now. At once. As soon as you can. For God's sake.'

He heard the quaver in her voice.

'Of course I'll come. Don't worry.'

What a comfort those two words were. She put down the receiver. She tried to think how long he'd be. It was more than three miles, much of it uphill, from the hotel to her villa. At that hour he wouldn't be likely to get a taxi; if he had to walk it would take him nearly an hour. In an hour it would be dawn. She could not wait in the room. It was horrible. She changed quickly from the wrap she was wearing into a dress. She turned out the light, unlocked the door, very cautiously in order not to make a sound, and slipped into the passage; she opened the front door and walked down the monumental stairway that led to the drive, then along the drive, keeping in the shade of the trees that lined it – for the moon, which before had filled her with such rapture, now, by the light it gave, terrified her – till she came to the gates. Here she stood. She was sick at heart when she thought of the interminable time she must still wait. But suddenly she heard footsteps, and panic-stricken she cowered back into the shadows. It was someone coming up the steep flight of steps which led from the bottom of the hill to the villa and which till the road had been made was its only means of access.

Whoever it was, was coming to the villa and seemed to hurry. A man came out of the darkness and she saw it was Rowley. Her relief was overwhelming.

'Thank God, you've come. How did you get here so quickly?'

'The night porter was asleep, so I borrowed his bike. I've hidden it at the bottom. I thought I'd get here more quickly by the steps.'

'Come.'

He peered into her face.

'I say, what's the matter? You look like hell.'

She shook her head. She couldn't tell him. She seized his arm and walked quickly back to the house.

'Be as quiet as you can', she whispered when they got inside. 'Don't speak.'

She led him to her room. She opened the door and he followed her in. She closed and locked it. For a moment she could not bring herself to turn on the light, but there was no help for it. She touched the switch. A great chandelier hung from the ceiling and at once the room was brilliantly alight. Rowley gave a violent start when his eyes fell on the body of a man lying on the floor near one of the two big windows.

'My God!' he cried. He turned and stared at her. 'What does it mean?'

'He's dead.'

'It looks damned well like it.'

He knelt and pulled down one of the man's eyelids, then, as Mary had done, put his hand on his heart.

'He's dead all right.' The revolver was still clasped in the man's hand. 'He killed himself.'

'Did you think I'd killed him?'

'Where are the servants? Have you sent for the police?'

'No', she gasped.

'But you must. He can't be left there. You must do something.' Mechanically, without thinking what he was doing, he loosened the revolver from the man's hand. He looked at it.

'That looks damned like the gun you showed me in the car.'

'It is.'

He stared at her. He couldn't understand. How could he understand? The situation was incomprehensible.

'Why did he shoot himself?'

'For God's sake don't ask me questions.'

'Do you know who he is?'

'No.'

She was pale and trembling. She looked as if she were going to faint.

'You'd better pull yourself together, Mary. No good getting jittery, you know. Wait a minute, I'll go along to the dining-room and get you some brandy. Where is it?'

He started to go, but with a cry she stopped him.

'Don't leave me. I'm afraid to stop here by myself.'

'Come along then', he said abruptly.

He put his arm round her shoulders to support her and led her from the room. The candles were still burning in the dining-room and the first thing he saw when he entered was what remained of the supper they had eaten, the two plates, the two glasses, the bottle of wine and the frying-pan in which Mary had cooked eggs and bacon. Rowley walked up to the table. By the side of the chair in which Karl had sat was his shabby felt hat. Rowley picked it up, looked at it and then turned to look at Mary. She could not meet his eyes.

'It wasn't true when I said I didn't know him.'

'That, I must say, is almost painfully obvious.'

'For God's sake don't talk like that, Rowley. I'm so terribly unhappy.'

'I'm sorry', he said gently. 'Who is he then?'

'The violinist. At the restaurant. The man who came round with the plate. Don't you remember?'

'I thought his face was vaguely familiar. He was dressed like a Neapolitan fisherman, wasn't he? That's why I didn't recognise him. And of course he looks different now. How did he happen to be here?'

Mary hesitated.

'I met him just as I was coming home. He was on the terrace half way up the road. He talked to me. He seemed so lonely. He looked terribly unhappy.'

Rowley looked down at his feet. He was embarrassed. Mary was the last woman in the world he would have expected to do what he could not but suspect that she had done.

'Mary dear, you know I'd do anything in the world for you. I want to help you.'

'He was hungry. I gave him something to eat.'

Rowley frowned.

'And after you'd given him a snack he just went and shot himself with your revolver. Is that the idea?'

Mary began to cry.

'Here, have a drink of wine. You can cry later.'

She shook her head.

'No, I'm all right. I won't cry. I know now it was madness, but it seemed different then. I suppose for a minute I was crazy. You know what I told you in the car, just before you got out.'

He suddenly understood what she meant.

'I thought it was a lot of romantic tripe. I never guessed you could be mad enough to do such a damn-fool thing. Why did he kill himself?'

'I don't know. I don't know.'

He reflected a minute and then began to gather the plates and glasses together and put them on the tray.

'What are you doing?' she asked.

'Don't you think it's just as well to leave no trace that you had a gentleman in to supper? Where's the kitchen?'

'Through that door and down a flight of stairs.'

He took the tray out. When he came back Mary was sitting at the table with her head in her hands.

'It's lucky I went down; you'd left all the lights on. You're evidently not used to covering up your tracks. Your servants hadn't washed up after their dinner. I just put the things with the rest. The chances are they won't notice. Now we must send for the police.'

She almost screamed.

'Rowley!'

'Listen to me, dear. You've got to keep your head. I've been thinking a lot and I'll tell you what I suggest. You must say that you were asleep and you were awakened by a man, obviously a burglar, coming into your room. You put on the light and snatched up the gun which was on the bed-table. There was a struggle and the gun went off. If you shot him or if he shot himself doesn't matter. It's probable enough that when he found himself cornered and was afraid your screams would bring along the servants he shot himself.'

'Who's going to believe a story like that? It's incredible.'

'Anyhow it's more credible than the truth. If you stick to it no one can prove it's a lie.'

'Nina heard the shot. She came along to my room and asked if anything was the matter. I said no. She'll tell them that when the police question her. How am I going to explain then? The story will fall to pieces. Why should I have told her nothing was the matter when a man was lying dead in my room? It's hopeless.'

'You can't bring yourself to tell me the truth?'

'It's so disgraceful. And yet – at the time – I thought I was doing something rather beautiful.'

She said no more and he stared at her, half understanding, but still puzzled. She gave a deep sigh.

'Oh, yes, let's send for the police and get it over with. It means ruin. Well, I suppose I've deserved it. I shall never be able to look anyone in the face again. The newspapers. And Edgar. That's the end of that.'

Then she said a surprising thing. 'After all, he wasn't a thief. I did him harm enough without casting a slur like that on the poor boy. I'm to blame for everything and I must take what's coming to me.'

Rowley looked at her intently.

'Yes, it means ruin, you're right there, and a hell of a scandal. You're in for an awful time, dear, and if it comes out nobody can help you. Are you willing to take a risk? I warn you, it's a great risk and if it doesn't come off it'll make it all the worse for you.'

'I'll take any risk.'

'Why can't we get the body away from here? Who could suspect then that his death had anything to do with you?'

'How can we? It's impossible.'

'No, it isn't. If you'll help me we can get him into the car. You know all these hills round here. We can surely find a place to put him where he won't be found for months.'

'But he'll be missed. They'll look for him.'

'Why should they? Who's going to bother about an Italian fiddler? He might have just done a bolt because he couldn't pay his rent, or run away with somebody else's wife.'

'He wasn't Italian. He was an Austrian refugee.'

'Well, that's all the better. Then you can bet your boots no one's going to make a song and dance about him.'

'It's an awful thing to have to do, Rowley. And what about you? Aren't you taking a fearful risk?'

'It's the only thing to do, my dear, and as far as I'm

concerned you needn't worry about that. To tell you the truth I rather like taking chances. I'm for getting all the thrills out of life one can.'

It heartened Mary to hear him speak so lightly. Her anguish seemed not quite so intolerable. There was just a hope that they might be able to do what he proposed. But one more doubt assailed her.

'It'll be light soon. The peasants will be setting out to their work as soon as it's dawn.'

He glanced at his watch.

'When does it get light? Not before five. We've got an hour. If we look sharp we can just manage it.'

She sighed deeply.

'I put myself in your hands. I'll do whatever you say.'

'Come on then. And keep a stiff upper lip for Christ's sake.'

Rowley picked up the dead man's hat and they went back into the room in which he was lying.

'Catch hold of the legs', said Rowley. 'I'll take him under the arms.'

They lifted him up and carried him into the hall and out of the front door. With difficulty, Rowley walking backwards, they got him down the steps. Then they put the body down. It seemed fearfully heavy.

'Can you bring the car up here?' asked Rowley.

'Yes, but there's no place to turn. I shall have to back down', she answered doubtfully.

'I'll manage that.'

She walked down to the end of the narrow drive

and brought the car up. Meanwhile Rowley went back into the house. There was blood on the marble floor, not much fortunately, because the man had shot himself through the breast and the hæmorrhage was internal.

He went into the bathroom, took a towel off the rack and soaked it in water. He mopped up the blood-stains. The floor was of a deep red marble and he was pretty sure that on a cursory glance, the sort of glance a maid would give who was sweeping, nothing would be apparent. He took the wet, blood-stained towel in his hand and once more went out. Mary was waiting by the car. She did not ask him what he had been doing.

Rowley opened the rear door and again put his arms under the dead man's. He hoisted him up and Mary, seeing he was having difficulty, lifted the feet. They did not speak. They laid the body on the floor and Rowley wrapped the towel round the dead man's middle in case the jolting caused a flow of blood. He jammed the soft hat on his head. Rowley got into the driving seat and backed down to the gates. Here there was plenty of room to turn.

'Shall I drive?'

'Yes. Turn to the right at the bottom of the hill.'

'Let's get off the main road as soon as we can.'

'About four or five miles along there's a road that leads up to a village on the top of a hill. I think I remember a wood on one side.'

When they came to the highway Rowley put on speed.

'You're driving awfully fast', said Mary.

'We haven't got much time to waste, my sweet', he said acidly.

'I'm so terribly scared.'

'That's going to do a fat lot of good.'

His manner was bitter and she was silent. The moon had set and it was very dark. Mary could not see the speedometer; she had a notion they must be doing hard on eighty. She sat with her hands clenched. It seemed an awful thing that they were doing, a dangerous thing, and yet it was her only chance. Her heart was beating painfully. She kept on repeating to herself:

'What a fool I've been!'

'We must have gone about five miles now. We haven't missed the turning, have we?'

'No, but we ought to be getting to it soon. Slow down a little.'

They went on. Mary looked anxiously for the narrow road that led winding up to the hill town. She had been along it two or three times, tempted by the sight of it in the distance, for it looked like one of those hill towns in the background of an old Florentine picture, one of those pictures of a scene from the Gospels which the painter has set in the lovely landscape of his native Tuscany.

'There it is!' she cried suddenly.

But Rowley had already passed it; he put on his brakes, and then backed till he could turn. They slowly ascended the hill. They peered into the darkness on each side. Suddenly Mary touched Rowley's arm. She pointed to the left. He stopped. There was a coppice on that side of what looked like acacias, and the ground was thick with undergrowth. It seemed to slope sharply down. He put out the lights.

'I'll just get out and have a scout round. It looks all right.'

He stepped out and plunged into the thicket. In the deathly silence that surrounded them the noise he made scrambling through the undergrowth seemed fearfully loud. In two or three minutes he appeared once more.

'I think it'll do.' He talked in whispers, although there could not have been a soul within earshot. 'Help me to get him out. I shall have to carry him if I can. You'd never be able to get down. You'd be scratched to pieces.'

'I don't care.'

'It's not you I'm thinking about', he answered roughly. 'How are you going to explain to your servants that your stockings are torn and your shoes in a devil of a mess? I think I can manage.'

She got out of the car and they opened the rear door. They were just about to lift the body out when they saw a light above them. It was a car coming down the hill.

'Oh, my God, we're caught!' she cried. 'Run, Rowley, you must keep out of this.'

'Don't talk such rot.'

'I *won't* get you into trouble', she cried desperately.

'Don't be a damned fool. We shan't get into trouble if you keep your head. We can bluff it out.'

'No, Rowley, for God's sake. I'm done for.'

'Stop it. You've got to keep cool. Get into the back.'

'He's there.'

'Shut up.'

He pushed her in and scrambled in after her. The lights of the oncoming car were hidden by a turn in the road, but another turn must bring it in full view.

'Cuddle up to me. They'll take us for lovers who've come to a quiet place to have a bit of nonsense. But keep still. Don't move.'

The car came on. In two or three minutes it would be upon them and the road was so narrow that it would have to slow down to pass them. It could just scrape by. Rowley flung his arms round her and drew her closely to him. Under their feet was the huddled body of the dead man.

'I'm going to kiss you. Kiss me as if you meant it.'

The car was nearer now and it seemed to be swaying from side to side of the road. Then they heard the occupants singing at the tops of their voices.

'By God, I believe they're drunk. I hope to God they see us. Christ, it would be bad luck if they hit us. Quick now, kiss me.'

She put her lips to his and they appeared to kiss as though so absorbed in one another they were unconscious of the approaching car. It seemed to be full of people and they were shouting loud enough to wake the dead. Perhaps there had been a wedding at the village on the top of the hill and these were wedding-guests who had been making merry till this late hour and now, much the worse for liquor, were returning to their own home in some other village. They appeared to be coming down the middle of the road and it looked as though they must infallibly crash into the other car. There was nothing to do. Suddenly there was a yell. The headlights had disclosed the stationary car. There was a great screeching of brakes and the oncoming car slackened down. It might be that the recognition of the danger he had just escaped somewhat sobered the driver, for he now drove at a snail's pace. Then someone noticed that there were people in the darkened car and when they all saw that it was a couple linked together in a passionate embrace a great laugh arose; one man shouted out a ribald joke and two or three others made rude noises. Rowley held Mary tight in his arms; you would have thought that in an ecstasy of love they were unconscious of all else. One bright spirit conceived an idea; in a rich baritone he broke out into Verdi's song from Rigoletto, 'La Donna è mobile', whereupon the rest, not knowing the words apparently, but anxious to join in, bellowed the tune after him. They passed the car very slowly; there was but an inch to spare.

'Throw your arms round my neck', whispered Rowley, and as the other car came abreast of them, his lips still against Mary's, he gaily waved his hand at the drunkards.

'Bravo! Bravo!' they shouted. 'Buon divertimento.' And then, as they went by, the baritone began once more to chant: 'La Donna è mobile'. . . They staggered dangerously down the hill, still lustily singing, and when they were lost to view their shouting could still be heard in the distance.

Rowley released his hold on Mary and she sank back, exhausted, into the corner of the car.

'It's a good thing for us all the world loves a lover', said Rowley. 'Now we'd better get on with the job.'

'Is it safe? If he were found just here . . .'

'If he's found anywhere on this road they might think our being in the neighbourhood was fishy. But we might go a long way and not find a better place and we haven't time to scour the country. They were drunk. There are hundreds of Fiats like this and what is there to connect us? Anyway, it would be obvious the man committed suicide. Get out of the car.'

'I'm not sure if I can stand.'

'Well, you'll damned well have to help me out with him. After that you can sit around.'

He got out and pulled her after him. Suddenly, flopping down on the running board, she burst into a passion of hysterical tears. He swung his arm and gave her a sharp, stinging slap on the face; she was so startled that she sprang to her feet with a gasp and stopped crying as quickly as she had begun. She did not even cry out.

'Now help me.'

Without a word more they set about what they had to do and together got the body out. Rowley picked it up under the arms.

'Now put the legs over my other arm. He's as heavy as hell. Try to pull those bushes aside so that I can get in without breaking them down.'

She did as he told her and he plunged heavily into the undergrowth. To her terrified ears the noise he made was so great that you would have thought it could be heard for miles. It seemed an interminable time that he was away. At last she saw him walking up the road.

'I thought I'd better not come out the same way as I went in.'

'Is it all right?' she asked anxiously.

'I think so. By God, I'm all in. I could do with a drink.' He gave her a look in which was the flicker of a smile. 'Now you can cry if you want to.'

She did not answer and they got back into the car. He drove on.

'Where are you going?' she asked.

'I can't turn here. Besides, it's just as well to drive on a bit so that there shouldn't be any trace of a car having stopped and turned here. Do you know if there's a road further on that will get us back on the main road?'

'I'm sure there isn't. The road just leads up to the village.'

'All right. We'll go on a bit and turn where we can.'

They drove for a while in silence.

'The towel is still in the car.'

'I'll take that. I'll chuck it away somewhere.'

'It's got the Leonards' initials on it.'

'Don't bother about that. I'll manage. If I can do nothing else I'll tie it round a stone and chuck it into the Arno on my way home.'

After they had gone another couple of miles they

came to a place where there was a bit of flat ground by the side of the road and here Rowley made up his mind to turn.

'Christ!' he cried, as he was about to do so. 'The revolver.'

'What? It's in my room.'

'I forgot all about it till now. If the man's found and they don't find the gun he killed himself with, it'll start them guessing. We ought to have left it by his side.'

'What's to be done?'

'Nothing. Trust to luck. It's been with us so far. If the body's found and no gun, the police will probably think that some boy had come upon the body by chance, sneaked the revolver and said nothing to anybody.'

They drove back as quickly as they had come. Now and then Rowley gave an anxious glance at the sky. It was night still, but the darkness had no longer quite the intensity it had had when they set out. It was not yet day, but you had a sensation that day was at hand. The Italian peasant goes to work early and Rowley wanted to get Mary back to the villa before anyone was stirring. At length they reached the bottom of the hill on which the villa stood and he stopped. Dawn was about to break.

'You'd better drive up by yourself. This is where I left my bike.'

He could just see the wan smile she gave him. He saw that she tried to speak. He patted her shoulder.

'That's all right. Don't bother. And look here, take

a couple of sleeping tablets; it's no good lying awake and grousing. You'll feel better after a good sleep.'

'I feel as if I'd never sleep again.'

'I know. That's why I say take something to make sure you do. I'll come round sometime tomorrow.'

'I shall be in all day.'

'I thought you were lunching with the Atkinsons. I was asked to meet you.'

'I shall call up and say I'm not well enough.'

'No. You mustn't do that. You must go, and you must act as though you hadn't a care in the world. That's only common prudence. Supposing by a remote chance suspicion fell on you, there must have been nothing in your behaviour to indicate a guilty conscience. See?'

'Yes.'

Mary got into the driver's seat and waited a moment to see Rowley get his bicycle from where he had hidden it and ride away. Then she made her way up the hill. She left the car in the garage, which was just within the gates, and then walked along the drive. She crept noiselessly into the house. She went up to her room and at the door hesitated. She hated to go in and for a moment was seized with a superstitious fear that when she opened the door she would see Karl in his shabby black coat standing there before her. She was distraught with woe, but she couldn't give way to it; she pulled herself together, but it was with a trembling hand that she turned the handle. She switched on the light quickly and gave a gasp of relief when she saw the room was empty. It looked exactly as it always did. She glanced at her bedside clock. It was not five. What fearful things had happened in so short a while! She would have given everything she had in the world to put time back and be once more the carefree woman she had been so few hours ago. Tears began to trickle down her face. She was terribly tired, her head was throbbing and confusedly she recollected, in one rush of memory as it were, everything happening simultaneously, all the incidents of that unhappy night. She undressed slowly. She didn't want to get into that bed again and yet there was no help for it. She would have to stay in the villa at least a few days more; Rowley would tell her when it would be safe to go: if she announced her engagement to Edgar it would seem very reasonable that she should leave Florence a few weeks sooner than she had planned. She forgot if he had said when he would have to sail for India. It must be quickly. Once there she would be safe; once there she could forget.

But as she was getting into bed she remembered the supper things that Rowley had taken into the kitchen. Notwithstanding what he had said she was uneasy and felt she must see for herself that everything was in order. She slipped on her dressing-gown and went down into the dining-room and so to the kitchen. If by any chance one of the servants heard her she could say that she had awakened hungry and had gone down to see if she could find something to eat. The house seemed fearfully empty and the kitchen a great gloomy cavern. She found the bacon on the table and put it back in the larder. She threw the broken eggshells into a pail under the sink, washed the two glasses and the plates she and Karl had used, and put them in their proper places. She put the frying-pan on its hook. There was nothing now to excite suspicions and she crept back to the bedroom. She took a sleeping draught and turned out the light. She hoped the tablets would not take long to act, but she was utterly exhausted, and while she was saying to herself that if she didn't sleep soon she would go mad, she fell asleep.

6

When Mary opened her eyes she saw Nina standing by her side.

'What is it?' she asked sleepily.

'It's very late, Signora. The Signora has to be in the Villa Bolognese at one and it's twelve already.'

Suddenly Mary remembered and a pang of anguish pierced her heart. Wide awake now, she looked at the maid. She was as usual smiling and friendly. Mary gathered her wits together.

'I couldn't get to sleep again after you woke me. I didn't want to lie awake the rest of the night, so I took a couple of my little tablets.'

'I'm very sorry, Signora. I heard a sound and I thought I'd better come and see if anything was wrong.'

'What sort of a sound?'

'Well, like a shot. I remembered the revolver that the Signore had left with you, and I was frightened.'

'It must have been a car on the road. At night sound travels so far. Get me a cup of coffee and then I'll have my bath. I shall have to hurry.'

As soon as Nina left the room Mary jumped up and went to the drawer in which she had hidden the revolver. For one moment she had been afraid that Nina had found it while she lay fast asleep and taken it away. Her husband Ciro could have told her at once that a chamber had been discharged. But the revolver was still there. While she waited for her coffee she reflected intently. She saw why Rowley had insisted that she should go to that luncheon party. There must be nothing in her behaviour that was not quite natural; for his sake now as well as for her own she must be careful. She felt infintely grateful to him. He had kept cool, he had thought of everything; who would have thought that that idle waster had so much grit in him? What would have happened to her if he hadn't kept his head when the drunken Italians in the car had come upon them at the most dangerous moment? She sighed. Perhaps he wasn't a very useful member of society, but he was a good friend; no one could deny that.

When Mary had had a cup of coffee and her bath, when she sat at her dressing-table and arranged her face, she began to feel much more herself. It was astonishing to see that notwithstanding what she had gone through, she looked no different. All that terror, all those tears had left no trace. She looked alert and well. Her honey-coloured skin showed no sign of fatigue; her hair shone and her eyes were bright. She felt a certain excitement steal over her; it gave her a kick to look forward to that luncheon where she would have to give a performance of high spirits and careless gaeity which would lead them all to say when she left: Mary was in wonderful form to-day. She had forgotten to ask Rowley if he had accepted the invitation he had said he had got; she hoped he would be there, it would give her confidence.

At last she was ready to go. She took a last glance at herself in the mirror. Nina gave her a fond smile.

'The Signora is looking more beautiful than I've ever seen her.'

'You mustn't flatter me so much, Nina.'

'But it's true. A good sleep has done you good. You look like a girl.'

The Atkinsons were middle-aged Americans who owned a large and sumptuous villa which had once belonged to the Medici, and they had spent twenty years collecting the furniture, pictures and statues which made it one of the show places of Florence. They were hospitable and they gave large parties. When Mary was shown into the drawing-room, with its Renaissance cabinets, its Virgins by Desiderio da Settignano and Sansovino, and its Perugino and Filippino Lippi, most of the guests were already there. Two footmen in livery were walking about, one with a tray of cocktails and one with a tray of things to eat. The women were pretty in the summer dresses they had been to Paris to buy, and the men, in light suits, looked cool and easy. The tall windows were open on a formal garden of clipped box, with great stone vases of flowers symmetrically placed and weather-beaten statues of the Baroque period. On that warm day of early June there was an animation in the air which put everyone in a good humour. You had a sensation that no one there was affected by anxiety; everyone seemed to have plenty of money, everyone seemed ready to enjoy himself. It was impossible to believe that anywhere in the world there could be people who hadn't enough to eat. On such a day it was very good to be alive.

Coming into the room Mary was acutely sensitive to the general spirit of cheerful goodwill that greeted her, but just that, that heedless pleasure in the moment, shocking her like the sudden furnace heat when you came out of the cool shade of a narrow Florentine street on to a sun-baked square, gave her a sharp, cruel pang of dismay. That poor boy was even now lying under the open sky on a hillside over the Arno with a bullet in his heart. But she caught sight of Rowley at the other end of the room, his eyes upon her, and she remembered what he had said. He was making his way towards her. Harold Atkinson, her host, was a fine handsome grey-haired man, plethoric and somewhat corpulent, with an eye for a pretty woman, and he was fond of flirting in a heavy, fatherly way with Mary. He was holding her hand now longer than was necessary. Rowley came up.

'I've just been telling this girl she's as pretty as a picture', said Atkinson, turning to him.

'You're wasting your time, dear boy', drawled Rowley, with his engaging smile. 'You might as well pay compliments to the Statue of Liberty.'

'Turned you down flat, has she?'

'Flat.'

'I don't blame her.'

'The fact is, Mr. Atkinson, that I don't like boys',

said Mary, her eyes dancing. 'My experience is that no man's worth talking to till he's fifty.'

'We must get together some time and go into this matter', answered Atkinson. 'I believe we've got a lot in common.'

He turned away to shake hands with a guest who had just arrived.

'You're grand', said Rowley in an undertone.

The approving look in his eyes encouraged her, but notwithstanding she could not help giving him a frightened, harassed glance.

'Don't let up. Think of yourself as an actress playing a part.'

'I always told you I had no talent for the stage', she answered, but with a smile.

'If you're a woman you can act', he retorted.

And that is what she did during the luncheon to which they soon sat down. On her right was her host, and she carried on with him a laughing flirtation, which amused and flattered him; and with her neighbour on the other side, who was an expert on Italian art, she talked of the Sienese painters. Society in Florence is not very large and several of the people were there who had been at the dinner the night before. Princess San Ferdinando, who had been her hostess, was on Atkinson's right. This occasioned an incident which nearly robbed Mary of her composure. The old lady leant across the table to address Mary.

'I was just telling the Count about last night.' She turned to Atkinson. 'I'd asked them to come and dine at Peppino's to hear a man who's got a marvellous voice and, would you believe it, he wasn't there!'

'I've heard him', said Atkinson. 'Mrs. Atkinson wants me to pay for his training. She thinks he ought to sing in opera.'

'Instead they had the most awful fiddler. I talked to Peppino. He says he's a German refugee and he only gave him a chance out of charity. He said he wouldn't have him again. You remember him, Mary, don't you? He was quite impossible.'

'He didn't play very well.'

She wondered if her voice sounded as unnatural to the others as it did to herself.

'That's putting it mildly', said the Princess. 'If I played the fiddle like that I'd shoot myself.'

Mary felt she must say something. She gave her shoulders a little shrug.

'It must be very difficult for people like that to find anything to do.'

'It's a bad business', said Atkinson. 'Young chap, was he?'

'Yes, hardly more than a boy', returned the Princess. 'He had quite an interesting head, hadn't he, Mary?'

'I didn't pay very much attention to him', she replied. 'I suppose they have to dress them up in those absurd clothes.'

'I didn't know he was a refugee. You know, now I feel rather badly about it. I suppose it's because I made such a fuss that Peppino said he'd fire him. I wonder if I could get hold of him, I might give him two or three hundred lire to carry on with till he finds another job.'

They went on talking about him interminably. Mary shot a distressed glance at Rowley, but he was at the other end of the table and did not see her. She had to cope with the situation alone. At last, mercifully, the conversation changed. Mary felt exhausted. She continued to talk of one thing and another, to laugh at her neighbour's jokes, to feign interest, to seem to enjoy herself; and all the time at the back of her mind, so vividly that it was like seeing a play on the stage, all the events of the previous night, from beginning to end, unfolded themselves before her tortured memory. She was thankful when she was at last able to get away.

'Thank you so much; it's been a lovely party. I don't know when I've enjoyed myself more.'

Mrs. Atkinson, white-haired, kind, shrewd and with a dry humour, held her hand.

'Thank *you*, my dear. You're so beautiful, you make any party a success; and Harold's had a grand time. He's a terrible old flirt.'

'He was very nice to me.'

'And so he should be. Is it true that we're going to lose you soon?'

Mrs. Atkinson's tone showed Mary that she was referring to Edgar. Perhaps the Princess had told her something.

'Who can tell?' she smiled.

'Well, I hope what I hear is true. You know, I look upon myself as a great judge of character. And you're not only beautiful, you're good and sweet and natural; I should like you to be very happy.'

Mary could not help the tears filling her eyes. She gave the kind lady a wan smile and quickly left.

7

When she got home a telegram, just arrived, was waiting for her:

Flying back to-morrow. Edgar.

The garden was terraced and there was one place in it for which Mary had a great affection. It was a little strip of lawn, like a bowling alley, surrounded by clipped cypresses, and on one side they had been cut into an arcade in order to give a view, not of Florence, but of an olive-clad hill on the top of which was a village with old red roofs and the campanile of a church. The spot was cool and sequestered and here Mary, lying on a long chair, sought peace. It was a relief to be alone and not to have to pretend. She could surrender herself now to her anxious thoughts. After some time Nina brought her a cup of tea. Mary told her she was expecting Rowley.

'When he comes, bring some whisky and a siphon and the ice.'

'Very good, Signora.'

Nina was a young woman who liked to gossip, and she had now a piece of news that she wanted to impart. Agata, the cook, had brought it up from the near-by village where she had her own cottage. Some of her relations there had let a room to one of those refugees who swarmed in Italy, and now he had run off, without paying for his board and lodging, and they were poor people and couldn't afford to lose the money. He'd never had anything but the clothes he stood up in, and the things he had left behind him wouldn't fetch five lire. They'd let him owe money for three weeks because he was so simpatico, and they were sorry for him, but it was a dirty trick to bolt like that; it was a lesson and it just showed that you were never repaid for the kindnesses you did people.

'When did he go?' asked Mary.

'He went out yesterday evening to go and play the violin at Peppino's – why, that was where the Signora dined last night; he said that when he came back he'd give Assunta money. But he never came back. She went down to Peppino's and they told her they knew nothing about him. He didn't give satisfaction and they said he needn't come again. But he had some money. You see, he got his share of the plate; one lady put in a hundred lire, and . . .'

Mary interrupted. She didn't want to hear any more.

'Find out from Agata how much he owed Assunta. I – I don't like the idea of her suffering because she did someone a kindness. I will pay.'

'Oh, Signora, that would be such a help to them. You see, with both their sons doing their military service and earning nothing, it's a job they have to keep going. They fed him, and food's expensive these days. It's us, the poor people, who have to suffer for making Italy into a great nation.'

'That'll do. You can go now.'

That was the second time that day that she had had to listen to someone speaking of Karl. Mary was seized with terror. It looked as though that unhappy man, whom no one bothered about while he was alive, now that he was dead was in some uncanny way calling attention to himself. A remark of the Princess's recalled itself. She had said that because she had been the cause of his losing his job she wanted to do something for him. She was a woman of her word and would seek him out; and she was an obstinate woman; if she could not find him she would move heaven and earth to discover what had become of him.

'I must get away from here. I'm frightened.'

If only Rowley would come! At the moment he seemed her only refuge. She had brought Edgar's wire in her bag; she took it out and read it once more. That was a way of escape. She began to think intently.

At last she heard her name called.

'Mary.'

It was Rowley. He appeared at the end of the grass plot and slouched towards her with his hands in his pockets; there was no elegance in his gait, but a lounging ease which in such a disreputable fellow would to some have seemed out of place, but which just then was strangely reassuring to Mary. He was entirely unruffled.

'Nina said I'd find you here. She's bringing along a

drink that I badly want. Jove, it's hot walking up that hill of yours.' He gave her a scrutinising glance. 'What's the matter? You don't look any too good.'

'Wait till Nina has brought the drinks.'

He sat down and lit a cigarette. When Nina came he chaffed her gaily.

'Now, Nina, what about all these babies that the Duce says every Italian woman should provide the State with? It doesn't look to me as though you were doing your duty.'

'Mamma mia, it's hard enough to feed oneself these days. How am I going to feed half a dozen brats?'

But when she was gone he turned to Mary.

'What is it?'

She told him of the incident at luncheon when the Princess had spoken of Karl and what Nina had just told her. He listened attentively.

'But, my dear, there's nothing in all that to get the wind up about. Jittery, that's what's the matter with you. He thought he'd got a permanent job and got fired; he owed his landlady money. He'd promised to pay her and hadn't got enough. Supposing he's found? He shot himself and he had plenty of motives.'

What Rowley said certainly sounded reasonable. Mary smiled and sighed.

'I suppose you're right. I've got the jitters. What should I do without you, Rowley?'

'I can't think', he chuckled.

'If we'd been caught last night – what would have happened to us?'

'We should have got it in the neck, dear heart.'

Mary gasped.

'You don't mean that we should have – gone to prison?'

He looked at her with smiling ironical eyes.

'It would have wanted a hell of a lot of explanation, you know. Two English people careering round the country with a corpse. I don't quite see how we could have proved he shot himself. Either you or I might have shot him.'

'Why should you?'

'A dozen reasons would occur to the fertile imagination of a cop. We went off together last night from Peppino's. People tell me that I haven't got the best reputation possible where women are concerned. You're an almost perfect specimen of the genus peach. How could we have proved that there wasn't something between us? I might have found him in your room and killed him out of jealousy; he might have caught us in compromising circumstances, and I might have killed him to save your reputation. People do these damn-fool things.'

'You were taking a most awful risk.'

'Don't mention it.'

'I was so upset last night I didn't even thank you. It was frightful of me. But I *am* grateful, Rowley. I owe everything to you. Except for you I think I should have killed myself. I don't know what I've done to deserve that you should do so much for me.'

He looked at her steadily for a moment and then gave a good-natured, casual smile.

'My dear, I'd have done it for any pal. I'm not

quite sure if I wouldn't even have done it for a total stranger. You know, I like risk. I'm not really a law-abiding person and I got a grand thrill out of it. Once at Monte I had a thousand pounds on the turn of a card, that was a thrill too; but nothing to this. By the way, where's the gun?'

'I have it in my bag. I dared not leave it in the house when I went out to lunch. I was afraid Nina would find it.'

He stretched out his hand.

'Let me have your bag.'

She did not know why he asked for it, but passed it over to him. He opened it, took out the revolver and put it in his pocket.

'Why are you doing that?'

He leaned back lazily in his chair.

'I take it that sooner or later the body will be found. 'I've been thinking it over and I believe it's better that the gun should be found with it.'

Mary smothered a cry of fright.

'You're not going back to that place?'

'Why not? It's a lovely afternoon and I want exercise badly. I rented a bike. There's no reason why I shouldn't ride along the high road and then have an impulse to take a side one with the idea of having a look at that picturesque village on the top of the hill.'

'Someone might see you go into the wood.'

'I shall certainly take the elementary precaution of looking about to see that no one is around.'

He got up.

'You're not going now?'

'I think so. As a matter of fact it's not much of a wood; I didn't tell you last night, because I thought you'd get more scared than ever, and there was no time to look further. I don't think you can expect that he won't be found pretty soon.'

'I shall live agonies till I know you're safely back again.'

'Will you?' He smiled. 'I'll look in on my way home. I dare say I shall be ready for another drink.'

'Oh, Rowley!'

'Don't be afraid. The devil's a sportsman and he looks after his own.'

He went off. To wait for him now was a torture such that beside it all she had gone through before seemed trifling. It was no good telling herself that compared with the risk which they had taken last night this was nothing; that, at the moment at all events, had seemed inevitable, but this was needless; he was putting his head in the lion's mouth for the fun of the thing, because he was getting pleasure out of exposing himself to danger. She grew on a sudden anger with him. He had no right to do such stupid things; she should have prevented him. But the fact was that when he was there taking it all in that breezy, humorous way, it was almost impossible to see things in their proper light. She had a feeling, moreover, that when he had made up his mind to do a thing it would need a great deal to dissuade him. A strange man. Who would have guessed that his flippant manner concealed so much determination?

'Of course he's been hopelessly spoilt', she said irritably.

At last he returned. She heaved a great sigh of relief. You had only to look at him, strolling jauntily towards her, a mocking smile on his lips, to know that everything had gone well. He threw himself in a chair and helped himself to a whisky-and-soda.

'That's a good job jobbed. There wasn't a soul in sight. You know, it looks at though chance went out of its way sometimes to give the criminal a helping hand. There was a little bit of a trickle of water just at the right place. I suppose there's a spring there and that's why there's all that undergrowth. I dropped the gun in it. In a few days it ought to be in a nice state.'

She wanted to ask him about the body, but could not bring herself to speak the words. They sat for a while in silence while he indolently smoked and with enjoyment sipped his cold drink.

'I should like to tell you exactly what happened last night', she said at last.

'You need not. I can guess the essentials and the rest doesn't much matter, does it?'

'But I want to. I want you to know the worst of me. I don't really know why that poor boy killed himself. I'm tortured with remorse.'

He listened without a word, his eyes, cool and shrewd, fixed on her, while she told him word for word all that had passed between her first sight of Karl, when he had stepped out of the shadow of the cypress, till the dreadful moment when the sound of the shot had startled her out of bed. Some of it was very difficult to tell, but with those steady grey eyes upon her she had an inkling that he would at once know if she concealed any part of the truth; it relieved her also to tell the story in all its shame. When she finished he leaned back in his chair and seemed intent on the smoke rings he was making with his cigarette.

'I think I can tell you why he killed himself', he said at last. 'He was homeless, outcast, penniless and half starved. He hadn't got much to live for, had he? And then you came. I don't suppose he'd ever seen such a beautiful woman in his life. You gave him something that in his wildest dream he could never have dreamt of. Suddenly the whole world was changed because you loved him. How could you expect him to guess that it wasn't love that had made you give yourself to him? You told him it was only pity. Mary, my dear, men are vain, especially very young men: did you never know that? It was an intolerable humiliation. No wonder he nearly killed you. You'd raised him to the stars and then you flung him back to the gutter. He was like a prisoner whose jailers lead him to the door of his prison and just as he is about to step out to freedom, slam it in his face. Wasn't that enough to decide him that life wasn't worth living?'

'If that's true I can never forgive myself.'

'I think it's true, but I don't think it's the whole truth. You see, he was unbalanced by all he'd gone through before, perhaps he wasn't quite sane; it may be that there was something else; it may be that you had given him a few moments of such ecstasy that he thought life after that could have nothing better to offer and so was willing to call it a day. You know, most of us have had moments in our lives when our happiness was so complete that we've said to ourselves: "O God, if I could only die now!" Well, he'd had that moment and that feeling, and he died.'

Mary looked at Rowley with amazement. Was it really he, the mocking, happy-go-lucky, reckless tough, who said such things! This was a Rowley that she had never known existed.

'Why do you say that to me?'

'Well, partly because I want you not to take it all too much to heart. There's nothing you can do about it now. The only thing is to forget, and perhaps what I've just told you will enable you to forget without misgiving.' He gave her the derisive smile which she knew so well. 'And partly because I've had several drinks and perhaps I'm a little tight.'

She did not answer. She handed him the telegram she had received from Edgar. He read it.

'Are you going to marry him?'

'I want to get away from here. I hate this house now. When I go into my room it's all I can do not to scream with horror.'

'And India's a long way off.'

'He has strength and character. He loves me. You see, Rowley, I've been taken down a peg or two. I want someone to take care of me. I want someone I can look up to.'

'Well, that settles that, doesn't it?'

She was not quite sure what he meant. She gave him a glance, but he was looking at her with smiling eyes which betrayed nothing.

She gave a faint sigh.

'But of course he may not want to marry me.'

'What the devil are you talking about now? He's crazy about you.'

'I must tell him, Rowley.'

'Why?' he cried, aghast.

'I couldn't marry him with this thing hanging over me. It would be on my conscience. I should never have a minute's peace.'

'Your peace? What about his peace? D'you think he'll thank you for telling him? I tell you everything's all right. Nothing can ever connect you now with the death of that wretched fellow.'

'I must be honest.'

He frowned.

'You're making a terrible mistake. I know these Empire-builders. The soul of integrity and all that. What do they know of indulgence? They've never had need of it themselves. It's madness to destroy his trust in you. He dotes on you. He thinks you perfect.'

'What is the good of that if I'm not?'

'Don't you think the better people think you are the better you're liable to become? You know, he's got many excellent qualities, your Edgar; they've got him where he is. But if you don't mind my saying so, he's got a certain obstinate stupidity; and that also has helped him. Without it he wouldn't be the big noise he is. You're asking something right out of his line when you're asking him to understand the labyrinth of a woman's sensibility.'

'If he loves me enough he will.'

'Very well, my dear, have it your own way. He's not the sort of cove I should want to marry if I were a woman, but if you've set your heart on him I suppose you must. But if you want to make a good job of it, take my advice and – emulate the clam.'

He gave a little chuckle, touched her hand lightly and with his jaunty step strolled away. The thought occurred to her that she might possibly never see him again. It gave her a slight pang. Funny he should have asked her to marry him. She had to smile at his dismay if she had taken him seriously and said she would.

8

It was about four next afternoon when Nina came out to Mary, again sitting in the garden and seeking to distract her mind by working on a piece of tapestry, and told her that Edgar Swift was on the telephone. He had just arrived at his hotel and wanted to know if he could see Mary.

She had not known at what time his 'plane would get in, and had been waiting for him since luncheon. She sent the message that she would be glad to see him whenever he cared to come. Her heart began to beat a trifle hurriedly. She took out her looking-glass from her bag and looked at herself. She was pale, but she did not put on any rouge, since she knew he did not much like it; she dabbed the powder-puff over her face and painted her lips. She was wearing a light summer dress, of yellow linen with a wall-paper design; it looked so simple that you would have thought a housemaid might have worn it, but it had been made by the best dressmaker in Paris.

Presently she heard the car drive up and a moment or two later Edgar appeared. She got up from her chair and advanced to greet him. As usual he was dressed perfectly as became his age and station. It was a pleasure to look at him as he strode along the strip of lawn; he was so tall and slim; he held himself so erect. He had removed his hat: his thick black hair shone with the oil he had put on to keep its wave set. His fine blue eyes below the thick eyebrows wore a friendly gleam; his fine, spare features no longer had the sternness which was his habitual expression, but were softened by a happy smile. He warmly clasped her hand.

'How cool and fresh you look, and as pretty as a picture.'

Mr. Atkinson had used that hackneyed phrase every time he saw her. Mary, faintly tickled to hear it from Edgar, supposed it was what gentlemen of a certain age always said to women much younger than themselves.

'Sit down and Nina will bring us some tea. Did you have a nice trip?'

'I'm so very glad to see you again', he said. 'It seems a century since I went away.'

'It hasn't been very long.'

'Luckily, I knew exactly what you'd be doing all the time. I knew where you'd be at such and such an hour and I followed you from place to place with my thoughts.'

Mary faintly smiled.

'I should have thought you were much too busy.'

'I was busy, of course; I had a couple of long talks with my minister and I think we've settled everything. I'm to sail at the beginning of September. He was very decent to me. He didn't conceal from me that it was a difficult job, though of course I knew that when I accepted it, but he said that was why they wanted *me*. I don't want to bore you with the compliments he paid me, but . . .'

'I want to hear. I shan't be bored.'

'Well, he said that owing to the particular circumstances, it was important to put a man there who was conciliatory and at the same time firm, and he was good enough to say that he knew no one who combined those qualities to so high a degree as I do.'

'I'm sure he was right.'

'Anyhow it was very flattering. You see, I've had a long fight and it's satisfactory to find oneself pretty near the top of the tree at last. It's a big job and an important one. It'll give me a chance to show what I can do, and between you and me and the gatepost, I think I can do a great deal.' He hesitated for an instant. 'And if I do as well as I hope, and as they hope, it may lead to even higher things.'

'You're very ambitious, aren't you?'

'I suppose I am. I like power and I'm not afraid of responsibility. I have certain gifts, and I'm glad of the opportunity to make the most of them.'

'There was a Colonel Trail at dinner the other night. He said that if you made a success in Bengal, there was no reason why you shouldn't become viceroy.'

A gleam came into Edgar's bold eyes.

'Governor-General, they call him now. I imagine that's within the bounds of possibility. They made Willingdon viceroy, and a damned good viceroy he was.'

They had finished tea and he put down his cup.

'You know, Mary, that the pleasure with which I'm looking forward to all this activity, and the honour that's attached to it, wouldn't mean half so much to me if I weren't hoping that you'd share it with me.'

Her heart stood still. The moment had come. To calm herself she lit a cigarette. She did not look at him, but she felt that his eyes, tenderly smiling, were fixed upon her.

'You promised to give me my answer when I came back.' He chuckled. 'The fact that I chartered a 'plane this morning to fly over here is proof that I'm impatient to have it.'

She threw away the cigarette she had just lit. She gave a little sigh.

'Before we go any further I've got something to tell you. I'm afraid it'll bitterly distress you. Please listen to me without saying anything. Anything you've got to say, any questions you've got to ask me, you can say later.'

His face on a sudden hardened and he looked at her sharply.

'I'll say nothing.'

'I don't have to tell you that I'd give anything in the world to hold my tongue, but I'm afraid it wouldn't be honest. You must know the facts and then do what you think fit.'

'I'm listening.'

Once again she told the long painful story which the day before she had told Rowley. She omitted nothing. She tried neither to exaggerate nor to minimise. But it was harder to tell it to Edgar. He listened without a movement. His face was set and stern. No flicker in his eyes showed what he was thinking. She was conscious as she spoke that her behaviour seemed more senseless and wanton than it had done when she was telling Rowley what had happened. She found it impossible to give her motives even a plausible air; some of the incidents appeared incredible and her heart sank as she imagined that perhaps he was not believing her. And now she realised that there was something peculiarly shocking in Rowley and her having placed the body in a car and taken it to hide in a sequestered spot in the hills. She still didn't know what else she could have done to avoid a fearful scandal and Heaven only knew what difficulties with the police. But it was so fantastic that anything like that should happen to people like her that it didn't seem to belong to real life; it was the kind of thing that happened to one in a nightmare.

At last she finished. Edgar sat quite still for a little while without saying a word, then he got up and began to pace to and fro across the green patch. His head was bent, he had his hands clasped behind his back, and on his face was a dark, sullen look that she had never seen on it before. He looked strangely older. At last he stopped still in front of her. He looked down at her and there was a painful smile on his lips, but his voice was so tender that it wrung her heart.

'You must forgive me if I'm rather taken aback. You see, you're the last woman I should ever have expected to do anything like this. I knew you when you were the most innocent, charming child; it seems incredible that you of all people . . .'

He stopped, but she knew what he had in mind; it seemed incredible that she of all people should have become the mistress of a casual vagabond.

'I have no excuses to make for myself.'

'I'm afraid I think you've been very foolish.'

'Worse.'

'We need not go into that. I think I love you enough to understand and to forgive.' There was a break in that strong man's voice, but his smile now was indulgent and gentle. 'You're a romantic, silly little thing. I can quite believe that what you did after that man killed himself seemed the only thing to do in the circumstances. It was an awful risk you took, but it appears to have panned out all right. The fact is, you badly need a man to look after you.'

She looked at him doubtfully.

'Do you still want to marry me now that you know everything?'

He hesitated, but for so brief a moment that to anyone but Mary it would have been unnoticeable.

'You surely didn't think I was going to leave you in the lurch? I couldn't do that, Mary dear.'

'I feel terribly ashamed of myself.'

'I want you to marry me. I will do everything I can to make you happy. Career isn't everything. After all, I'm not so young as I was. I've done a good deal for the country; there's no reason why I shouldn't sit back now and let younger men have a chance.'

She stared at him with sudden perplexity.

'What *do* you mean?'

He sat down again and took her hands in his.

'Well, darling, you see this does alter things a bit. I couldn't take on this job; it wouldn't be fair. If the facts leaked out the effects might very well be disastrous.'

She was aghast.

'I don't understand.'

'Don't bother about it, Mary dear. I'll telegraph to the minister to say that I'm going to be married and so can't go to India. I can make your health a very reasonable pretext. I can't offer you quite the same position as I'd hoped, but there's no reason why we shouldn't have a very good time. We can take a house on the Riviera. I've always wanted a boat of my own. We can have a lot of fun sailing about and fishing.'

'But you can't throw everything up just when you're reaching the top of the tree. Why should you?'

'Listen to me, dear. It's a very ticklish job I've been offered; it needs all my intelligence and all my serenity. I should always have the anxiety that something might be discovered. You're not at an advantage to make a calm and considered judgment when you're standing on the crater of a volcano.'

'What can be discovered now?'

'Well, there's the revolver. The police could find out if they took the trouble that it had belonged to me.'

'I dare say they could. I've thought of that. It might be that the man had taken it out of my bag at the restaurant.'

'Yes, I have no doubt one could think of a variety of plausible ways how he might have got hold of it. But there'd have to be explanations, and I can't afford to have it necessary to make explanations. I don't want to put on any frills, but I'm not the sort of man to tell a pack of lies. And then it's not only your secret. It's Rowley Flint's as well.'

'You can't suppose for a moment that he'd ever give me away.'

'That's just what I can suppose. He's an unscrupulous scamp. An idler. A waster. He's just the sort of man that I have no use for. How do you know what he'll do when he's had a couple? It's too good a story to waste. He'll tell it in confidence to some woman. He'll tell one and then he'll tell another, and before you know where you are it'll be all over London. Believe me, it won't take long then to reach India.'

'You're wrong, Edgar. You misjudge him. I know he's wild and reckless, if he hadn't been he'd never have taken that risk to save me, but I know I can trust him. He'll never give me away. He'd rather die first.'

'You don't know human nature as I do. I tell you he hasn't got it in him to resist telling the story.'

'But if you think that it would be just the same if you'd retired or not.'

'There might be a lot of gossip, but if I'm in a private position what does it matter? We can snap our fingers at it. But it would be very different if I were Governor of Bengal. After all, what you did is a criminal offence. For all I know it's extraditable. It would be a fine chance for an unfriendly Italy to sling mud. Has it occurred to you that you might be accused of killing the man yourself?'

He stared at her so sternly that she shuddered.

'I've got to play fair', he went on. 'The Government has trusted me and I've never let them down. In the position they want to put me in it's essential that nothing can be said about my character or my wife's. Our situation in India largely depends now on the prestige of its administrators. If I had to resign in disgrace it might be the occasion of the most serious events. It's no good arguing, Mary; I must do what I'm convinced is right.'

His tone had gradually changed and his voice was as harsh as his expression was stern. Mary saw now the man who was known all through India not only for his administrative ability but for his ruthless determination. Watching every line of his grim face, intent on the flicker of his eyes which might disclose his real feelings to her, she sought to discern his inmost thoughts. She knew very well that he had been shattered by her confession. He was incapable of sympathy for such outrageous, such shocking behaviour. She had destroyed his belief in her and he would never again feel quite sure of her. But he was not the man to take back the offer he had made. When of her own free will she had told him what she might easily have kept to herself, he could do nothing but respond to her frankness with generosity; he was prepared to sacrifice his career and the chance of making a great name for himself, to marry her; and she had an inkling that he took something like a bitter joy in the prospect of such a sacrifice, not because he loved her so much that it was worth while, but because his sacrifice heightened his pride in himself. She knew him well enough to know that he would never reproach her because on her account he had had to give up so much; but she knew also that with his energy, his passion for work and his ambition, he would never cease to regret his lost opportunities. He loved her and it would be a cruel disappointment not to marry her, but she had something more than a suspicion that now he would give her up, however unhappily, if it were humanly possible to do so without a surrender of his self-respect. He was the slave of his own integrity.

Mary lowered her eyes so that he should not see the faint gleam of amusement in them. Strangely enough, the situation struck her as slightly diverting. For she knew now, quite definitely, that whatever the circumstances, even if nothing had happened that he need be afraid of, even if he were made Governor-General of India to-morrow, she didn't want to marry him. She was attached to him, she was grateful because he had taken the unhappy incidents she had felt bound to tell him so kindly, and if she could help it she did not want to hurt his feelings. She must go warily. If she said the wrong thing he would grow obstinate; he was quite capable of overruling her objections and marrying her almost by main force. Well, if the worst came to the worst, she would have to sacrifice whatever remained of the good opinion he had of her. It was not very pleasant, but it might be necessary; and if then he thought the worst of her, well, that would make it the easier for him.

With a sigh she thought of Rowley; how much easier it was to deal with an unscrupulous scamp like that! Whatever his faults, he was not afraid of the truth. She pulled herself together.

'You know, Edgar dear, it would make me miserable to think that I'd ruined this distinguished career of yours.'

'I hope you'd never give it a thought. I promise you that when I'd retired into private life I shouldn't.'

'But we oughtn't only to think of ourselves. You're the man for this particular job. You're needed. It's your duty to take it regardless of your personal feelings.'

'I'm not so conceited as to think I'm indispensable, you know.'

'I've got such a very great admiration for you, Edgar. I can't bear the thought of you deserting your post when your presence is so necessary. It seems so weak.'

He gave a little uncomfortable movement and she felt that she had caught him on the raw.

'There's nothing else to do. It would be even more dishonourable to accept the position under the circumstances.'

'But there is something else to be done. After all, you're not obliged to marry me.'

He gave her a look so fleeting that she could not be sure what it meant. He knew that, of course, and did that look mean: Good God, if I could only get out of it, don't you think I would? But he had great control over his expression and when he answered his lips were smiling and his eyes were tender.

'But I want to marry you. There's nothing in the world I want more.'

Oh, well then, she'd got to take her medicine.

'Edgar dear, I'm very fond of you. I owe so much to you; you're the greatest friend I've ever had. I know how splendid you are, how true and kind and faithful; but I don't love you.'

'Of course I know that I'm a great many years older than you. I realise that you couldn't love me in quite the same way as you'd love a fellow of your own age. I was hoping that, well, the advantages I had to offer would in some measure compensate for that. I'm dreadfully sorry that what I have to offer you now isn't perhaps so much worth your accepting.'

God, how difficult he was making it! Why couldn't he have said right out that she was a slut and he'd see her damned before he married her? Well, there was the cauldron of boiling oil; there was nothing to do but to shut one's eyes and jump right in.

'I want to be quite frank with you, Edgar. When you were going to be Governor of Bengal, you would have had a lot of work and I should have had a lot too; after all, I'm human and the position was dazzling; it seemed enough if I liked you. We should have had so many interests in common, it didn't seem to matter if I wasn't in love with you.' Now the most difficult part was coming. 'But if we're just going to live a quiet life on the Riviera, with nothing much to do from morning till night, well, I think the only thing that would make it possible would be if I were as much in love with you as you are with me.'

'I'm not set on the Riviera. We could live anywhere you liked.'

'What difference would that make?'

He was silent for a long time. When he looked at her again his eyes were cold.

'You mean that you were prepared to marry the Governor of Bengal, but not a retired Indian civilian on a pension.'

'When it cames down to brass tacks I suppose that is really what it amounts to.'

'In that case we need not discuss the matter further.'

'There doesn't seem much point in doing so, does there?'

Again he was silent. He was very grave and his face showed no indication of what he was thinking. He was humiliated, poor man, and bitterly disappointed in her, but at the same time Mary was pretty sure he was infinitely relieved. But that was the last thing he proposed to let her see. At last he hoisted himself out of his chair.

'There seems no object in my staying in Florence any longer. Unless, of course, you'd like me to stay in case there's any bother over – over that man who killed himself.'

'Oh, no, I think that's quite unnecessary.'

'In that case I shall go back to London to-morrow. Perhaps I had better say good-bye to you now.'

'Good-bye, Edgar. And forgive me.'

'I have nothing to forgive.'

He took her hand and kissed it, then with a dignity in which there was nothing absurd walked slowly down the grass patch and in a moment was hidden by the box hedge. She heard his car drive away.

9

The interview had tired Mary. She had had no natural rest for two nights and now, lulled by the smoothness of the summer air and the monotonous, pleasant chattering of the cicadas, the only sound that disturbed the silence, she fell asleep. In an hour she woke refreshed. She took a stroll in the old garden and then made up her mind to sit on the terrace so that she could look again at the city below her by the lovely light of the declining day. But as she passed the house Ciro, the manservant, came out to her.

'Signor Rolando is on the 'phone, Signora', he said.

'Ask him to leave a message.'

'He wishes to speak to you, Signora.'

Mary shrugged her shoulders slightly. She did not particularly want to speak to Rowley just then; but it occurred to her that he might have something to tell her. The thought of that poor boy's body lying on the hillside was always on her mind. She went to the telephone.

'Have you got any ice in the house?' he said.

'Is it to ask me that you made me come to the 'phone?' she answered coldly.

'Not entirely. I wanted to ask you also if you had any gin and vermouth.'

'Anything else?'

'Yes. I wanted to ask if you'd give me a cocktail if I got into a taxi and came along.'

'I've got a lot to do.'

'That's fine. I'll come along and help you.'

Shrugging her shoulders a trifle irritably, Mary told Ciro to bring what was wanted to make a cocktail and went out on to the terrace. She was eager to get away from Florence as quickly as possible. She hated it now, but she did not want her departure to arouse comment. Perhaps it was just as well Rowley was coming; she would ask him. It was rather absurd, when you came to think of it, that she should rely so entirely on someone who was so notoriously unreliable.

Fifteen minutes later he was with her. It was a strange contrast he made with Edgar as he walked across the terrace. Edgar, with his height and his spareness, had looked wonderfully distinguished; he had a natural dignity and the assured air of a man who had been accustomed for many years to the obedience of others. If you had seen him in a crowd you would have asked who that man was whose face was so full of character and whose manner bespoke authority. Rowley, rather short, rather stocky, wearing his clothes as though they were a workman's overalls, slouched across, with his hands as usual in his pockets, with a kind of lazy impudence, debonair and careless, which, Mary was bound to admit, had a certain attractiveness. With his smiling mouth and the good-humoured mockery of his grey eyes, of course not a person you could take seriously, but one who was easy to get on with. It suddenly occurred to Mary why notwithstanding his faults (and disregarding the great service he had rendered her) she felt so much at ease with him. You could be entirely yourself. You never had to pretend with him, first because he had a keen eye for any sort of humbug and only laughed at you, and then because he never pretended himself.

He mixed himself a cocktail, drank it in a gulp and then sank comfortably into an armchair. He gave her a roguish look.

'Well, darling, so the Empire-builder's turned you down.'

'How d'you know?' she asked quickly.

'I put two and two together. When he came back to the hotel he asked about trains and when he found he could catch the Rome-Paris Express to-night he ordered a car to take him to Pisa. I surmised that if it hadn't been a bust he would hardly have left with such precipitation. I told you it was stupid of you to spill the beans. You couldn't expect a man like that to swallow that story of yours.'

It was no good making a tragedy of it when Rowley took it so flippantly. Mary smiled.

'He behaved very well.'

'He would. I'm sure he behaved like a perfect gentleman.'

'He is a perfect gentleman.'

'Which is a damned sight more than I am. I'm a gentleman by birth, but not by nature.'

'You don't have to tell me that, Rowley.'

'You're not sore, are you?'

'I? No, I don't ask you to believe me, but the truth is that as we talked it all over I came to the conclusion that I wouldn't marry him at any price.'

'You're well out of it. I didn't want to say too much as you seemed so set on marrying him, but you'd have been bored to death. I know women. You're not the sort of woman to marry an Empire-builder.'

'He's a great man, Rowley.'

'I know he is. He's a great man posing as a great man. That's what's so fantastic about him. It's like Charlie Chaplin impersonating Charlie Chaplin.'

'I want to get away from here, Rowley.'

'I see no reason why you shouldn't. A change will do you good.'

'You've been very kind to me. I shall miss you.'

'Oh, but I think we shall see a great deal of one another in the future.'

'What makes you think that?'

'Well, because as far as I can see there doesn't seem much else for you to do but to marry me.'

She sat up and stared at him.

'What *do* you mean?'

'Well, a lot has happened since then and I daresay it's slipped your memory, but I did make you a proposal of marriage the other night. You don't suppose I took your answer as final. So far, every woman I've asked to marry me always has, you know.'

'I thought you were joking. You couldn't really want to marry me now.'

He sat back in the armchair, smoking a cigarette,

a smile on his lips and a twinkle in his good-natured eyes; and his tone was so casual that you would have thought he was indulging only in badinage.

'You see, my dear, the advantage of me is that I'm a bad hat. A lot of people reproach me for the things I've done; I dare say they're right; I don't think I've done anyone much harm, women have liked me and I have a naturally affectionate disposition, so the rest followed almost automatically; but anyhow I've got neither the right nor the inclination to reproach other people for what *they've* done. Live and let live has been my motto. You see, I'm not an Empire-builder, I'm not a man of character with an unimpeachable reputation, I'm just an easy-going chap with a bit of money who likes to have a good time. You say I'm a rotter and an idler. Well, what about reforming me? I've got an estate in Kenya and I'm sacking my manger because he's no good; I've been thinking it mightn't be a bad idea if I went out and managed it myself. Perhaps it is about time that I settled down. You might like the life there.'

He waited a moment for her to speak, but she said nothing. She was so surprised and all he said was so unexpected that she could only look at him as though she scarcely understood. He went on, talking with a slight drawl, as though what he was saying were rather funny and he expected her to be amused by it.

'You know, you were quite right in saying that at first I only wanted to have an affair with you. Well, why not? You're very beautiful. I should be a funny sort of cove if I hadn't wanted to do something about you. But the other evening when we were driving you said one or two things that rather touched me. I couldn't help thinking you rather sweet.'

'A lot of things have happened since then.'

'I know, and I don't mind telling you that at one moment I was very angry with you.'

She gave him a glance from under her eyelashes.

'Is that why you hit me?'

'When you got out of the car, d'you mean? I hit you because I wanted you to stop crying.'

'You hurt me.'

'That was the idea.'

Mary looked down. When she told Edgar what had passed between her and that unfortunate boy, his face had gone grey with anguish. He had been profoundly shocked. But she had felt that what afflicted him was that she could thus have sullied the purity which he so prized in her; the truth was that he loved not the woman she was now, but still the pretty little girl to whom he gave chocolates and who had fascinated him by her ingenuous and childish innocence. It was the sexual jealousy of the male, baulked in his desire, that had caused Rowley to give her that vicious blow; it was odd what a strange, proud feeling it gave her suddenly to know that. She could not help giving him a look in which there was the suspicion of a smile. Their eyes met.

'But I'm not angry with you any more. You see, I liked your sending for me when you were in a hell of a mess. And then the way you kept your head, it looked pretty sticky at one moment; you've got nerve all right and I liked that too. Of course you behaved like a perfect idiot. But it showed you had a generous heart, and to tell you the truth, not many of the sort of women I've known had that. I love you terribly, Mary.'

'How strange men are!' she sighed. 'Both of you, Edgar and you, attach so much importance to something that really doesn't very much matter. What really matters, what wrings my heart, is that that poor, friendless boy through my fault should lie dead and unburied under the open sky.'

'He's just as well off there as in a cemetery. You can't bring him back to a life he had no use for by grieving over him. What does he mean to you really? Nothing. If he passed you in the street to-morrow you probably wouldn't even recognise him. Clear your mind of cant. That's what Dr. Johnson said, and damned good advice it was.'

She opened her eyes wide.

'What on earth do you know about Dr. Johnson?'

'In the leisure moments of an ill-spent life I've read a good deal. Old Sam Johnson is rather a favourite of mine. He had a lot of common sense and he knew a thing or two about human nature.'

'You're full of unexpectedness, Rowley. I would never have thought you read anything but the sporting news.'

'I don't keep all my goods in the shop window', he grinned. 'I don't think you'd find it so boring to be married to me as you might suppose.'

She was glad to find a flippant remark.

'How on earth could I ever hope to keep you even moderately faithful?'

'Well, that would be up to you. They say a woman ought to have an occupation, and that would be a very suitable one for you in Kenya.'

She looked at him for a moment reflectively.

'Why should you bother to marry me, Rowley? If you love me as much as you say I don't mind coming for a trip with you. We can take the car and go for a tour in Provence.'

'That's a suggestion, of course. But it's a damned rotten one.'

'There doesn't seem much object in exchanging a good friend for an indifferent husband.'

'That's a nice thing for a respectable woman to say.'

'I'm not so respectable as all that. Don't you think it's rather late for me to put on frills?'

'No, I don't. And if you start getting an inferiority complex I shall give you such a hiding as you won't forget for a month. It's marriage lines for me, my dear, or nothing. I want you for keeps.'

'But I don't love you, Rowley.'

'I told you the other night, you will if you give yourself half a chance.'

She looked at him for some time, doubtfully, and then suddenly the gleam of a shy but faintly teasing smile stole into her lovely eyes.

'I wonder if you're right', she murmured. 'The other night, in the car, when those drunken people passed us and you held me in your arms, though I was scared to death, I don't mind admitting that while your lips were pressed to mine the sensation wasn't – entirely unpleasant.'

He gave a great throaty chuckle. He jumped up and dragged her to her feet and flung his arms round her. He kissed her on the mouth.

'So now what?'

'Well, if you insist on marrying me. . . But it's an awful risk we're taking.'

'Darling, that's what life's for – to take risks.'

Also available in Vintage

W. Somerset Maugham

THE MOON AND SIXPENCE

'Art is a manifestation of emotion, and emotion speaks a language that all may understand.'

Inspired by the life of Paul Gauguin, *The Moon and Sixpence* tells the story of Charles Strickland, a conventional stockbroker who abandons his wife and children for Paris and Tahiti, to live his life as a painter. Whilst his betrayal of family, duty and honour gives him the freedom to achieve greatness, his decision leads to an obsession which carries severe implications. *The Moon and Sixpence* is at once a satiric caricature of Edwardian mores and a vivid portrayal of the mentality of genius.

Also available in Vintage

W. Somerset Maugham

CAKES AND ALE

'They did not behave like lovers, but like familiar friends... her eyes rested on him quietly, as though he were not a man, but a chair or a table.'

Cakes and Ale is the book that roused a storm of controversy when it was first published. It is both a wickedly satirical novel about contemporary literary poseurs and a skilfully crafted study of freedom. It is also the book by which Maugham most wanted to be remembered – and probably still is.

As he traces the fortunes of Edward Driffield and his extraordinary wife Rosie, one of the most delightful heroines of twentieth century literature, Maugham's sardonic wit and lyrical warmth expertly combine in this accomplished and unforgettable novel.

'A formidable talent, a formidable sum of talents...precision, tact, irony, and that beautiful negative thing which in so good a writer becomes positive – total, but *total* absence of pomposity'

Spectator

BY W. SOMERSET MAUGHAM
ALSO AVAILABLE IN VINTAGE

☐ CAKES AND ALE	£6.99
☐ OF HUMAN BONDAGE	£9.99
☐ THE MOON AND SIXPENCE	£6.99
☐ THE RAZOR'S EDGE	£6.99

- All Vintage books are available through mail order or from your local bookshop.
- Payment may be made using Access, Visa, Mastercard, Diners Club, Switch and Amex, or cheque, eurocheque and postal order (sterling only).

☐☐☐☐☐☐☐☐☐☐☐☐☐☐☐☐

Expiry Date:_______________ Signature:______________________________

Please allow £2.50 for post and packing for the first book and £1.00 per book thereafter.

ALL ORDERS TO:

Vintage Books, Books by Post, TBS Limited, The Book Service,
Colchester Road, Frating Green, Colchester, Essex, CO7 7DW, UK.
Telephone: (01206) 256 000
Fax: (01206) 255 914

NAME:______________________________

ADDRESS:______________________________

____

____

Please allow 28 days for delivery. Please tick box if you do not wish to receive any additional information ☐
Prices and availability subject to change without notice.